Roadtrip for ~~ONE~~ TWO

Roadtrip Romance • Book Two

AMY R. ANGUISH

Scrivenings
PRESS
Quench your thirst for story.
www.ScriveningsPress.com

Published by Scrivenings Press LLC
15 Lucky Lane
Morrilton, Arkansas 72110
https://ScriveningsPress.com

Printed in the United States of America

Paperback ISBN 978-1-64917-258-7

eBook ISBN 978-1-64917-259-4

Editors: Shannon Vannatter and K. Banks

Cover by Linda Fulkerson, bookmarketinggraphics.com

All characters are fictional, and any resemblance to real people, either factual or historical, is purely coincidental.

This book goes out Whitney Mitchell, Jonathan and Demeree Whitt, and Cassie Henley, who helped me out the few times I got to explore Dallas for myself over the years. I love you all and appreciate all you did for us when we were in that big city.

1

"No. No, no, no."

That voice. It sliced through Bree Henley's heart sharper than any knife, reverberating pain she thought had finally subsided. But no. Her throat tightened, and she squeezed her eyes shut, willing the strength for this encounter.

She glanced up from her paperback despite knowing who stood there. How could she not? She was supposed to be here with him—back before he'd called everything off. Nathan Hart, her ex-fiancé.

In his plaid button-up and grey pants, he looked just as handsome as ever. She'd always had a thing for slightly nerdy guys, and his glasses and rumpled hair fit the bill from the moment she'd spotted him across a mutual classroom during their sophomore year of college. Too bad he'd decided he couldn't trust her.

"Hello to you too." Somehow her words came out normal instead of shaky like her insides.

"What are you doing here?" He motioned to the hard plastic airport seat she occupied.

"Traveling." She crossed her legs, hoping to appear nonchalant. "You?"

"Bree, be serious. There's no way you're here in the same airport I am without something being up."

"No? I suppose you'll go all Humphrey Bogart on me and ask why out of all the airports in all the world, I had to pick yours? Though I didn't realize you owned this one." She glanced over her shoulder at the hustle inhabiting DFW. "It's nice."

His jaw tightened as if holding back words. "Please tell me we're not headed to the same place."

"Unless you tell me where you're going, I can't answer that. Although I'd say it's a fairly safe bet, all things considered." She pulled a ticket from the front pocket of her purse, using the time to swallow one last lump of emotion. "This says Houston."

"The cruise?"

"The cruise." She lifted a brow. "Though why you chose to book a cruise, I don't understand. I thought we'd agreed to go to New York City."

He glanced around, and then his shoulders slumped, and he slid into a seat next to her. "You wanted to go to New York City. I didn't care where we went. And this was cheaper."

"Cheaper? You managed to find a cruise around the Caribbean cheaper than a week in New York City?" She shook her head. "And you call me the travel guru."

He tensed, and she realized she'd just opened old wounds again. The ones that cut him much deeper than she'd expected. Enough for him to decide he didn't trust her enough to go through with their wedding. The wedding that should have happened the day before, back in Tennessee.

She ran a thumbnail around the left-hand finger, still

missing the ring that'd lived there for over a year. He wasn't the only one with unhealed wounds.

"Who gave you the information to be able to take this trip?" He crossed his arms and kept to the far edge of his chair as if afraid of touching her. "And how did I not see you on the flight from Nashville?"

"Skye said she got it from Josh. And he helped me change my flight to one out of Memphis since that's where I'm living right now." Bree tucked her ticket back in its place and glanced over at the screen announcing loading times. Weren't they supposed to leave soon?

"Josh." Nathan groaned his brother's name. "I should've known. Let me guess. Skye said you should take the trip, that I couldn't get a refund anyway, and it might as well not be wasted?"

"Pretty much." Almost exactly, in fact. Skye and Katie had told her it would be a great way to work through her depression over the relationship falling apart. Soak up some sun, maybe even meet someone new. She'd never believed the last part, but the sun and waves had sounded good. Not to mention all the desserts probably on board. Hadn't even thought to ask if Nathan might be going too.

And now they had a whole week to look forward to being trapped on a boat—wait! Would they have to be in the same room? Part of her considered backing down now, but why should she be the one to give up this trip? He was the one who didn't want to be with her.

"They set us up." The words escaped his lips as more of a growl.

"I guess Josh basically gave you the same spiel?"

"Yep. And stupid me, I bought it hook, line, and sinker. You know I can't stand to waste money."

"So, you were going on the cruise by yourself?"

"I for sure wasn't taking Josh." Nathan scoffed. "My baby brother can be a lot of things, but he's not who I want next to me on a cruise."

She nodded, though his words sliced her already wounded heart. Apparently, she wasn't who he wanted next to her on a cruise either.

"And you were going by yourself?"

She motioned around to prove there was no one else with her.

He opened his mouth, but static crackled before the intercom kicked on.

"Flight 453 to Houston has been canceled due to weather."

"Canceled!" Nathan jumped up, knocking over his carry-on. "I have to find another flight. I'm supposed to meet the ship this afternoon."

Bree's gaze wandered to a nearby television, something she'd paid no attention to earlier. She tugged on his sleeve. Unless she was mistaken, there wouldn't be another flight. And probably not a cruise, either.

"Bree, I have to go talk to the lady at the counter."

"Look." She pointed to the screen.

A huge red blob swirled off the coast of Texas, orange and green spinning off it and covering most of the state. How had she missed hearing about a hurricane? Not to mention not noticing the rain lashing the windows around them.

"Something tells me that cruise isn't leaving Houston today."

Nathan slumped down into the seat once more. "So much for not wasting money."

"Won't they give you any of it back? I mean, I know they wouldn't let you cancel for a ... when our original plans fell through." She pinched her lips together for a second before charging forward. "But surely they can't hold the weather against you."

He nodded once. "There's a clause about natural disasters. But it might take me a few days."

"At least you won't have to worry about losing your money." She wrapped her arms around her middle. What now? She should probably see if there were any flights back to Memphis, where she'd been rooming with Katie while she figured out her new life plan.

"Guess I better see about finding a way back to Nashville." He rose once more.

So much for their friends' and brother's good intentions. The odds just didn't seem to be in favor of this relationship working. Bree stifled a sigh and took a deep breath. Time to put those dreams aside for good. Though it wouldn't be easy after nurturing them for several years.

The more she thought about going back right away, the more depressing it seemed. She'd meant to take this whole week and spend it relaxing and having fun. Why should she let a hurricane ruin that? There was still plenty to do elsewhere. The options were endless—as long as she didn't mind using her credit card.

She grabbed a travel magazine off the table next to her. One that happened to be for Texas. The serendipity wasn't lost on her. As she flipped through pages of cowboys and local flora, several bright photos caught her eye. Dallas. Why not? She'd never been here before. Why not stay a few days and explore?

Might as well take the lemons thrown at her and make some lemon squares. Maybe she'd even buy a pair of boots.

"Nothing at all?" Nathan leaned as far over the counter as he dared. There had to be something leaving DFW today. At this point, he didn't even care which direction it was headed.

"I'm sorry, sir." The employee shook her head. "The hurricane is spinning storms off all across the state, and we're actually under a tornado watch right now. Possibly a tornado warning for Dallas county in the next hour. Nothing is taking off until this mess gets past us. My best suggestion is to take the hotel voucher, get some rest tonight, and we can try again tomorrow."

"A whole day lost." He stepped back and shook his head. "This has to be the worst honeymoon in the history of the world." Especially since it wasn't technically a honeymoon.

"I'm sorry, sir. I can't control the weather." The worker glanced past him at the people waiting for him to make up his mind.

"Let me talk to my fian—Bree. Let her know we're stuck for now."

"Of course. I'll be here when you're ready."

He took a few steps back toward Bree and stopped. It wasn't actually his responsibility to let her know an update. He'd had no plans of taking this cruise with her—not since calling off the wedding. Besides, she was an old hat at planning trips, considering all those road trips she'd taken with Skye and Katie. She was ahead of him when it came to figuring this out.

And wasn't that one of the reasons he'd ended it? Not because of her travel acumen, but because he wasn't good enough for her. And the more they'd fought while she traveled all over the south with Skye and Katie a month ago, the more he'd realized things would only grow worse. Especially if they lived together every day, in the same apartment, while trying to make him into something he had no idea how to be.

Bree glanced up, her dark brown hair falling away from her face. Those blue eyes that used to crinkle at the edges with a smile just for him now met him in an icy stare. He couldn't walk away without telling her something.

"What's up? Get a flight?" She closed a magazine and set it down as he approached.

"Nope." He sank back into one of the chairs. "The hurricane is causing problems in more than just Houston, evidently. There's some tornadic weather close by, and all flights are delayed until things calm down. She offered a hotel voucher for the night and said I might be able to fly out tomorrow."

"Bummer." Bree pulled her phone out and started searching for something on the internet.

"What are you looking for?"

"First, I'll try and get a refund for my flights. Then I thought I'd see about finding a hotel and a rental car."

"A rental car? You won't need a car if you stay at the hotel here at the airport. That's what the voucher is for."

"No offense, Nathan, but I don't want to stay at the airport hotel. I want something closer to downtown so I can explore and play tourist." She pressed the phone to her ear and started answering the questions of whoever had answered.

Play tourist? Here? By herself?

He should just walk away. Nothing held him to her anymore. He'd ended that a month ago. And yet a war raged in his chest, volleying excuses, guilt, and frustration back and forth at the thought of abandoning her to a strange, big city in the middle of a thunderstorm and possible tornadoes.

She was still his friend—at least in theory. And a fellow Christian. Should he at least try and talk some sense into her?

"Perfect. Yes. Thank you so much. You too." Bree ended her call and gathered her things.

"Where are you going?"

"To see about renting a car and finding a place to stay for a few days. I've never been to Texas before, so I plan to soak up as much of it as I can this week."

"Bree, wait." He caught her arm and warmth shot through him at the contact.

Slowly, her eyes shifted to meet his, slightly wider than they'd been a few moments before. The noise of the airport faded away as if they were in their own bubble. What was going on? He wasn't supposed to still be attracted to her. And then she blinked and reality crashed around him again.

Her shoulders dipped slightly, as if he were a heavy load she bore. "What, Nathan?"

"I'm just not sure it's safe for you to run around all over Dallas by yourself."

"I'm an adult. I mean, I was old enough to be planning a wedding a few months ago. Old enough to be a college graduate. Old enough to move out of my parents' place and get a job. People travel by themselves all the time. I'll be fine, but thank you for your concern."

"Seriously, Bree. What if something happened to you?"

She shook her head, grabbed her suitcase, and took off down the concourse. He snatched his own things and speed walked after her, dodging mothers with clingy children, oblivious tourists, and suited businessmen. How had she gotten so far in such a short amount of time?

Her eyes barely cut his way as he fell in beside her. "Are you following me?"

"I feel responsible." Why was he winded when she wasn't?

"Why?" She stopped in the middle of traffic, causing some unkind words to be thrown her way. "There's no reason to. It wasn't your choice that landed me here today. You gave up the right to feel responsible when you called off the wedding.

You're free. Go ... do whatever it is you want to do now." She flicked her hands at him and started walking again.

"I don't know what I'll do yet, so at least let me make sure you safely get to your rental car."

A huff that would've done an elephant proud escaped her cute lips. "Fine."

Nothing else, but he'd take it. Though why he felt it was a victory, he had no idea. She was right. He didn't have to look after her anymore.

He blinked and noticed she'd pulled ahead, so he picked up the already frantic pace, hopping on the escalator right behind her to head down to the rental car area. What he'd do after that, he had no idea. Staying in an airport hotel held no attraction for him. Texas had never been on his bucket list to visit, though, so staying didn't sound great either.

She paused and perused the different companies. Did she know which were better, cheaper, safer? Had she ever rented a car before?

As if realizing she looked uncertain, she pointed herself toward one and took off again. He noticed it boasted lower prices and nodded his approval before following. The man behind the desk offered a smile and rose to shake her hand.

"Let me guess. Your flights were canceled?" He chuckled. "We're getting a lot of that today."

"Flight and cruise." Bree flashed him a grin. "I don't have anything else to do, so I figure I'll just explore Dallas for a few days."

"Well, welcome to our beautiful city. It's not usually as wet as it is today." He chuckled at his own joke. "What are you looking to rent? We don't have a ton of options right now because of how many people are bypassing the grounded planes, but we do have a few left."

"I don't need anything fancy. Just something to get around in."

Nathan winced at her ignorant words. She would end up with the lousiest model the place had. Would it even go a whole week without breaking down or leaving her stranded?

"Okay, let me pull up my inventory. Meanwhile, I'll need your driver's license and insurance information, please."

Bree started rummaging in the giant yellow bag she called a purse, finally pulling out her bright blue wallet. Nathan pressed his fingertips to his temple. Why was he even down here? Wouldn't it be better to let her take care of herself and not think about it anymore? If they hadn't both been conned into taking the cruise, he wouldn't be worrying about her right now. Not much, anyway.

"You, too, sir." The clerk pointed at Nathan.

"I'm sorry?"

"I need your license and insurance, too."

"No—I'm–"

"We're not—"

He and Bree both broke off as they protested at the same time.

"Oh, I'm terribly sorry. I assumed you were together. I'll be with you in just a minute." He turned back to Bree. "Can you wait a moment? I need to check with my associate on something."

"Of course." Bree nodded.

Nathan sighed. This day just got better and better. What else could possibly go wrong? He'd gone from looking forward to some sun and good food to standing in the basement of the airport in a rain-soaked Dallas with no plans for either. With his ex-fiancée.

The clerk returned and showed Bree the options, talked her through the fee she'd have for being under twenty-five—her reaction had him stifling a chuckle—and all the restrictions and rules that went along with it. Bree nodded and signed all the appropriate lines, then whipped out a credit card. So irresponsible. Had she even found a job yet?

"Sir?" A firm voice behind him caught Nathan's attention. He turned and found two airport security guards looking at him as if he were a thief.

"Yes?" Nathan swallowed a lump of shock. What was going on?

"We need to ask you a few questions."

2

He should know better. Should remember not to ask what else could go wrong. He'd never had security guards corner him like a criminal before. And it definitely wasn't something he'd wanted to experience.

"Okay. I can answer questions." He kept his hands out to show they were empty. "What's this about?"

"We got a report that you were stalking and acting suspiciously." The officer on the left shifted, tucking his thumbs in his belt loops as if to emphasize the Taser strapped there.

"Stalking?" Was this guy for real? Did they mean Bree?

"Sir, now calm down. We can talk about this up in our office where it's more private." Mr. Right-Side moved a few steps closer, and Nathan inched back.

"But I wasn't stalking. Ask Bree. She'll tell you."

He looked her way, hoping against hope that she wasn't still mad at him. She stood, half facing the counter still, mouth agape, as his drama played out behind her. If her eyes got any bigger, they'd roll out of her head. Would her shock lift in time to help him out?

"Let's just walk this way and we'll talk about it, okay? That's all we're going to do. We're not arresting you or anything." Beltstrap clapped a hand on Nathan's shoulder and nudged.

"Well, I should hope you're not arresting me. I haven't done anything wrong." Nathan considered digging in his heels but then changed his mind—that might make him look guiltier. Though how he looked guilty at all, he couldn't fathom.

He'd just been trying to help Bree. Was that so wrong? Was the universe suddenly against him in every aspect of his life? If he thought it would do any good, he'd blame his dad for this catastrophe, too, but he didn't have time to figure out all the connections to make it work.

"Nathan?" Bree's voice finally called out behind him, now that the two guards had walked him fifteen yards toward the escalators.

"Bree, I guess I'm headed this way for now." Nathan craned his neck to answer her, but the officers wouldn't let him turn enough to actually make out more than her long, brown hair.

Several more steps. If he got on that escalator, what would he face? How could he prove he wasn't stalking her? He had been standing fairly close and watching her more than anything. Maybe it looked bad. But bad enough to report him? That must've been what the car rental clerk had done when he stepped into the back of his office space.

Why had Nathan let Josh talk him into this trip? He hadn't wanted to come. Not really. Not without ... not without the one he planned to share it with in the first place. The one who was letting him get dragged off for stalking her in the airport. Didn't they have a better relationship than that, despite everything?

"Wait!" Bree's voice was breathless, but it was closer than it had been. "Wait, please!"

One guard kept his hand on Nathan's shoulder; the other turned to see what was going on behind them. "How can I help you, Miss?"

"He wasn't stalking me."

"He wasn't?" Mr. Beltstrap pushed his hat back on his head. "It sure looked suspicious when we walked up. And if it hadn't looked a little hairy, Barry over there wouldn't have called it in."

"I know it didn't look normal, but it's a long story." Bree pushed a wayward strand of hair off her forehead. "I promise. You don't have to keep escorting him away. He didn't mean anything bad towards me."

"And how can we know that?"

"I wouldn't try to save someone who was stalking me, would I?" Bree propped her fists on her hips and got that sassy look that always warmed his middle. Still worked, even in this insanity.

"So, you know this guy?" The man holding Nathan peered around him and motioned with a fat finger.

"Yes. I know him. He's my ..." Her eyes darted up and met his, and in that moment of hesitation, he knew his whole week was about to change once again. "... fiancé."

She left off the *ex*. Why had she done that? To convince these goons they were together? Her pause hadn't made it very convincing, though it shattered a bit of his heart to hear it again.

"Your fiancé?" Mr. Right-Side shifted and raised a brow. "You don't sound so sure."

"Sorry. The ... relationship status ... is a bit new." She pulled out her phone and punched something before holding the screen for the officer to see.

"And this is?"

"Our engagement photos." She tucked her left hand behind that giant purse and pointed with her right. "See?"

"Well, it at least proves you know each other enough to take pictures together." He handed back the device, and the other guy eased his grip. "Are you sure you're okay?"

"Perfectly fine. Thank you so much for your concern, but it really is unneeded." She flashed a giant smile his way.

"Okay, buddy. You better thank your fiancée that she's willing to vouch for you. But if we see you in here again following another pretty girl around, we won't hesitate to walk you off and ask those questions we had." The officer thumped his arm, and then they stalked off.

Nathan's legs felt about as solid as marshmallow fluff. He glanced around and headed toward the first seat he could find, sliding down onto the hard plastic and sinking his head into his hands. Maybe if he squeezed his eyes closed hard enough, when he opened them again, everything would be normal—no airport, no hurricane, no Bree, no crazy rental car clerk who thought he looked shady.

Nope. He blinked. He was still here in la-la land. If this was what Texas was like, he wasn't sure he liked it.

"That was ... close." Bree perched on a seat beside him.

"That's one word for it. *Insane*, *surreal*, and *terrifying* are others that come to mind."

She hummed her agreement but said nothing else.

His brain raced back to the claim she'd used to help clear him. "Your fiancé, huh?"

"At least until we can get out of this airport." Her expression could only be called sheepish. "It was the only thing that came to mind."

"I can't believe you still had those photos on your phone. Or that they didn't notice your lack of a ring." He slumped down in the seat, a mixture of relief and adrenaline loss making his spine curl.

"I thought about deleting them the other day." She played with a loose thread on the edge of her suitcase. "I just couldn't do it. Not yet."

He nodded. For the first time in a long time, he had no idea what to do with his current situation. And it choked his need to be in control.

"So, what now?" He straightened again, leaning forward, elbows on knees. "What's your plan? Rent a car and see Dallas, then fly home?"

Bree shook her head. "I canceled my flights, remember? I plan to drive home. Turn this into a road trip. It's what I do best, right? Of course, since I set Katie up with Camden and Skye is off to see her sister in Colorado, I'll have to figure out how to do it solo this time."

A fire crept into his throat as she oh-so-casually mentioned one of the reasons he'd ended their relationship in the first place. Had she forgotten how it hurt him? How her last adventure caused so many fights only a month before?

Bree knew the moment Nathan got angry again. His whole demeanor shifted, his spine straighter than she'd seen it this whole time, his jaw like iron, his blue eyes like steel. What had she said? Was it because of Camden?

And here she'd thought they were doing well, all things considered. Sort of. If you didn't count him being upset at her being here in the first place, or the canceled cruise, or the tornadoes in the area, or the whole stalker episode. So, maybe not the greatest moment in their history.

"You plan to just pick up some random guys on this trip

too? Let them follow you all the way back?" Nathan's voice was as cold as his posture.

"I told you." She turned to face him more fully. Maybe without a computer screen between them, he'd finally understand. "I didn't pick up random guys during our trip last month. Camden was interested in Katie, and Ryan just wanted to have fun with Skye. Neither of them paid me any attention. The only guy I wanted to talk to each evening was you, and as soon as you found out about them, all you wanted to do was fight."

"You think I *wanted* to fight?" His voice screeched, and he cut a look back towards the car rental place where this mess began. He calmed the tone and leaned toward her. "I don't understand how you can blame me for this."

"Because you didn't trust me." She poked his shoulder. "You promised me forever. Said we'd get married and make everything work out. And then you called it off for no good reason."

"No good reason?" He brushed her hand away.

"Yes. No good reason. Because I had no interest in those guys and they had no interest in me. In fact, when you saw Camden that Saturday, if you'd paid any attention at all, you'd have seen he only had eyes for Katie. And we left Ryan in Atlanta. But you didn't believe me." The last few words slipped out in a little whine as the ache festered in her chest, but she couldn't pull it back. She didn't want to—he needed to know he'd hurt her.

He opened his mouth, then closed it again, leaning back against the seat. What went through his head? Had she finally convinced him? Was he concocting some other arbitrary argument? What was the point of all this?

"You want me to trust you?" The question was barely a whisper, but she heard it.

"You can't have a relationship without trust. I thought I had yours, but you proved me wrong." She slid the strap of her bag back up on her shoulder and stood.

"Show me." He came out of his seat too.

"What?"

"Show me what it was like to have guys tagging along on your road trip. I was never invited on one, but you let those strangers join what was supposed to be your bachelorette fling. So, I'll join this one."

"You can't just join my road trip." She put a hand on her hip and eyed him warily. Now she really didn't know what was going through his head. This was nothing like the Nathan she'd known in college.

"Why not?" He motioned around as if to imply she had no other options for passengers.

"Because, for one thing, I'm not with Katie and Skye this time. And for another thing, you're not a stranger following me. We know each other. Have a history. It's nothing like what happened a month ago. Besides, if you were like them, you'd be interested in Katie or Skye."

"No." He shook his head. "Let's just pretend I'm a stranger and I see you the first day of your trip. And then what happens? Tell me how it worked."

She pinched her lips together, wondering at the sense in this idea. Was he trying to work his way back to her? Or trying to justify his actions? Either way, the stubborn streak that ran the full length of her five-foot-two frame kicked in. She'd prove him wrong.

"Fine." She planted her feet. "I guess the first two nights, you'd stay in the same hotel but some other room. Then, when I left for my next location, you'd secretly find out where it was so you could follow. You'd stay at a separate location that night. Then, the following day, you'd find a way to discover we were once again traveling in the same direction, and you'd join me there and then take me to one of my favorite pastimes.

"And that would basically be it unless you wanted to act more like Ryan than Camden. In which case, you'd cause trouble the next day and make everyone mad."

She bit back the words she wanted to add—that maybe he was more like Ryan. He wasn't. Somewhere deep inside this man was the guy she'd fallen in love with over old movie screenings on campus, school plays, study sessions, and dreams of what might be. Something had happened after graduation to change that, but she couldn't figure out what it was.

"How about we just start with the first day? We'll rent a car and find a hotel where we can get separate rooms. Then, you can show me how you explore a town and find all the fun things to do you always talked about on your road trips."

"Rent a car together?"

"Might as well save some money, right?"

"Did you cancel your flights?" Something held her back, and she scrambled to find more obstacles to keep this plan from happening.

"I didn't, but I will. Let's get the car situation worked out first, and then we can find somewhere else to go before I make those calls. I don't exactly love the ambiance here." He glanced around as if scared someone else would misjudge his intentions.

"Um, okay." She shifted and grabbed her suitcase handle. "But maybe we pick a different rental place?"

A chuckle escaped him as he bent over to pick up his bag. "Fine with me."

So, they were really going to do this. Take a road trip together even though officially they weren't supposed to be spending this week together at all.

Because they hadn't gotten married the day before.

What had she just agreed to? It was like the worst joke of a honeymoon she could imagine. And no telling what might happen by the end of the week.

If there was one thing she'd learned from her multiple trips with Skye and Katie, it was that you felt one of two ways about your buddies by the end—you hated them, or you loved them more than ever. Could her still-wounded heart take this risk? Could she prove she was still the woman he'd wanted to spend forever with?

3

It took them a while to decide which rental place to use and which car to pick. Because why should they suddenly start getting along just because they agreed to do this road trip together? Bree paused at the passenger door like she always had. And then reminded herself they were no longer engaged in real life—or even dating.

She slid in, hoping he wouldn't notice her hesitation. But when she glanced up, he stood on her side anyway, looking a bit lost. Had he come over to open her door? What was going on with him? He'd been so adamant about breaking it off with her, and now he almost acted like he wanted another chance.

Would she be willing to give him one? She hadn't wanted to end their engagement and was still picking up the pieces of her broken heart. It couldn't handle much more.

"So, where to now?" He slid behind the steering wheel.

She blinked away from her worries and into the present. "Lunch?"

"Sounds good to me." He cranked the engine and eased out

of the spot. "You look something up on GPS, and I'll get us there."

"Burgers?"

"Sure."

She called out directions as he squinted through the deluge the wipers could barely hold at bay. Several times they almost missed a turn because he couldn't tell if a car was behind them or not. But thirty minutes later, they'd fought their way into Dallas proper and were parked by an orange-and-white fast-food joint.

The rain fell in sheets, but neither had an umbrella. Rain hadn't been in her plans when she decided to take this trip. Nor had staying here.

He shot her a guilty glance. "Sorry I can't offer a jacket or anything."

"I think we should just run for it." She put a hand on the door handle. "On the count of three?"

She counted fast and darted out into the downpour before he could get his door open. Puddles splashed behind her as he followed on her heels. Inside the entryway of the restaurant, Bree stood giggling and dripping on the black rug. He stepped in beside her and shook his arms off, for all the good it did.

"Remember that time we got caught in a downpour on the far side of campus and had to run back through the rain and change clothes before we could head to dinner?" The memory hit her like a blanket just out of the dryer—warm at first but cooling quickly.

"I remember." From the tone of his voice, it affected him the same way.

That had been a good day. They'd been so far away because he'd been working up the nerve to propose. The weather had gone from partly cloudy to a thunderstorm in a matter of moments and overtook them all the way down the street on a walk with no car nearby. They'd hoofed it back, splashing and soaked in seconds, barely making it up the hill to her dorm before collapsing in laughter.

Some people might not want a wet proposal, but she couldn't imagine anything more perfect than him brushing her hair back outside her dorm lobby, pressing a kiss to her forehead, and whispering he wanted to do life with her. He'd barely been able to wiggle the ring out of his drenched pocket, but when he did, it slid on perfectly and sparkled under the raindrops.

Why had *that* memory been the one to pop up now? Besides the obvious rain, it was lousy timing. She pushed aside the melancholia that threatened to close off her throat and pointed to the menu.

"Want to start looking at the options? I'm going to see if there are paper towels or an air dryer in the bathroom."

"I'll do the same."

She pressed the silver button on the dryer in the bathroom and contorted her body to get as much as possible under the pitiful stream of air. It would take forever for her to dry off this way. And there wasn't a paper towel in sight. They would just have to suck it up and be miserable until they could find a dry place to stay.

After ordering, they claimed a booth near the restaurant's back corner, and Bree considered sliding over next to him on the bench. The shared warmth was tempting. But not appropriate for people supposedly only friends.

"Maybe we should find a hotel while we eat?" Bree pushed her hair off her neck where it clung. "If nothing else, it would be a dry place to spend the afternoon and plan the rest of the week."

He nodded in agreement but kept his focus on the little

plastic number that would tell the worker where to bring his food.

"I found several options within easy driving distance of the downtown area. I figured I probably wouldn't venture too far away from here." She hovered her finger over the tiny map of Dallas on her phone.

"I'm not really sure where *here* is, but what you said makes sense."

Their food arrived before she could reply. Of course, she wouldn't earn his trust that quickly, but it would've been nice for him to say he thought she knew what she was doing or something. At least he admitted her points were valid.

He swirled his fries in a mixture of ketchup and mustard and took a bite. "Did you find a job yet?"

The change in subject threw her off for a minute, but she recovered and shook her head. "Nothing full-time, but hopefully soon. Until then, I'm teaching kids overseas early in the mornings for a cushion to help pay rent and such."

"But you're willing to run up a bill on your credit card this week anyway? Even not having a real way to pay it off?" He took a big bite of burger, seemingly unaware—or maybe unconcerned—that he basically just called her irresponsible and stupid in so many words.

"I told you. I'm working the online teaching gig right now." It was enough to pay off the parts of their wedding she couldn't get refunded. She pulled an onion off her burger. "And if I need to make a little more to pay for this, I can take on a few extra students. Why do you care, anyway? I'm not your responsibility."

The arrow hit its mark—she could tell. His wince was more than from the pickle on his sandwich. Though it didn't leave her with a sense of accomplishment or gain. She'd cared about him too long to want to cause him pain.

"If you're worried about money, you can try to find something cheaper, but I checked several sites, and these were the lowest across all of them. And this one has a code where you can get ten percent more discounted." She shoved her phone across the table and pointed to the hotel.

"I guess it's been a while since I stayed in a hotel. I had no idea they ran so high." He pushed it back.

"But at least you'll get your money back from the cruise. And your flights."

***

"True." Shouldn't be too hard. After all, he'd been able to book the trips with just a few clicks. He finished off his lunch and wadded up the paper. "I'll work on that after we figure out where we're going."

"Depending on check-in time, you might want to just make those calls here instead." She tapped the entry she'd mentioned earlier and showed they weren't allowed to get a room until three. It was only one now.

"Nothing is ever easy, is it?" He let out a deep breath.

"You're welcome to call in the car if you want more privacy, but this place is fairly deserted thanks to this beautiful weather. And you'd have to run through the rain again to get there." Bree hooked a thumb over her shoulder toward the parking lot.

"Hmm. Run through the rain to get even wetter and sit in a car, or stay here already wet in the frigid air conditioning." He mimed weighing the options in his upturned palms. "Not really a win-win situation today."

"Sorry." She munched an onion ring, and he was glad they weren't kissing anymore. At least, he told himself he was. He was glad to not have to deal with onion breath, anyway.

He pulled up all the information for the flights and called the number listed. As he waited forty-five minutes for the clerk to pull up and cancel his flight information, his choice of being an accountant instead of a travel agent was confirmed. And sadly, that was probably the easier of the two to fix.

"Looks like you need a pick-me-up." Bree pushed a cup of coffee and a fried pie his way. "It's lemon, so I knew you'd want to try it."

His favorite. Of course, she wouldn't forget all the little things she'd learned about him over the last three years just because he'd called off the wedding. But it still caught him off guard that she'd go the extra steps to get it for him. Something that felt a lot like remorse tried to worm its way up through his gut, but he washed it back down with a swig of the coffee. No time for regret right now.

"If the radar is right, we might get a bit of a break in the next half hour. If we do, I say we run for it and try to get to the hotel before this mess starts again." Bree tapped her chin as she studied the screen in front of her.

"I'm on board with that."

"Ha. I see what you did there." She smirked.

He blinked a few times. "What?"

"On board? Like we were going to be on board a cruise ship, but now we're on board with just trying to beat the rain and get to a cheap hotel?" She lifted one brow and quirked her head to the side.

"O-kay." He stretched the word out. While they'd seen eye to eye on most things, sometimes her sense of humor didn't quite align with his.

"Anyway, do you want to wait to call about the cruise until after that? It took a while with the airlines, and I wasn't sure about the other."

He nodded around a mouthful of pie, which was much better than he expected.

"Okay, then." She played with a napkin, tearing it into strips, never looking up with those blue eyes of hers.

Would their whole trip be like this? Going from moments where they were okay straight to moments of awkward silence immediately after? Before her last road trip, they'd been able to talk about anything, fill hours with conversation, never have any seconds where discomfort set in. He'd ruined that. Or she had, by taking that stupid vacation.

"Oh, look." She pointed out the window.

A few beams of sunshine shot through the clouds, highlighting the sporadic drips still falling and making them sparkle. His chest loosened. Okay. Maybe it was a sign of better things to come. There was even a tiny rainbow struggling to form across the grey sky.

"Better go now." He quickly gathered the bit of trash left and dumped it in the canister on the way out of the restaurant.

This time, he beat her to her side and pulled the door open for her. She cast him a glance he couldn't interpret before sliding in. Couldn't he still be a gentleman even if he wasn't anything special to her?

She called the hotel on the way and confirmed an early check-in so they didn't have to wait in the parking garage and let the rain catch back up before heading in. It wasn't anything fancy—nothing he would've booked for a honeymoon trip. But he reminded himself he wasn't on a honeymoon. This was just a road trip with a friend.

"How many nights?" The clerk asked Bree.

She glanced over her shoulder at him. "We didn't decide that, did we?"

"It's Saturday. So, if we stay three nights, that puts us leaving Tuesday. Four would be Wednesday. Five Thursday."

He ticked days off on his fingers. "And you're still wanting to drive back across Arkansas too."

"Right. I think we can explore enough in three days, don't you?"

"So, four nights?"

"Oh." She tapped her forehead. "Right. Because today doesn't count since we can't go far, huh?"

"Right."

"Four nights, please."

The clerk glanced between the two of them and then nodded and typed it into the computer. "You're all set."

They ended up with rooms right next to each other. And when they got inside, there was a door connecting the two. Something told him that wouldn't open over the next few days. Double bed, television set, a chair and table, simple bathroom, and a window that looked down on a parking lot. Home sweet home for now.

The walls were thin enough that he could hear Bree's voice on the other side, though he couldn't make out any words. Was she talking to herself or on the phone? Letting someone know she was safe?

Maybe he ought to call Josh and let him know what he thought about this little trick of convincing Bree to go on the same trip he'd convinced Nathan to take. Some brother he was. If Josh ever broke up with Haven, man, Nathan was ready to give some payback.

Just what had his brother and Skye expected to happen in this situation? Granted, this wasn't the plan their friends had started with. No. They'd wanted them trapped on a boat together for a whole week. And in that scenario, they'd be sharing a cabin too. At least this way, he got a room to himself, bare as it was.

Bree's voice rose and fell. She must be on the phone. With Katie? Skye? Her mom?

Used to be, she'd talk to him like that. Spill out everything she'd gone through or felt. Who took his place in that area? And why did he care?

He unpacked a few things from his bag before sitting down to start the battle with the cruise line. From the very first automated voice that answered the phone, he dreaded the rest of this call.

"Speak. To. A. Rep-re-sent-a-tive!" Nathan tried to enunciate each syllable.

"I'm sorry. I didn't quite catch that. Please say your answer again." The system sounded friendly enough, but he'd love to punch it. "If you'd like to ..."

On the fourth try, he finally got, "Please hold one moment while I connect you to our customer service representatives."

"Finally." He propped his feet up on the bed and crossed his ankles.

"Your call is very important to us. We're sorry for the inconvenience, but we're experiencing high call volume right now. All our customer service representatives are busy helping other customers. If you'd like to stay on the line ..."

He let out a growl. Of course they were getting lots of calls. A hurricane had ruined the departure of their cruise. But that didn't mean he wanted to wait another forty-five minutes before even getting to talk to someone, which would probably take at least that much longer. A glance at his watch had him wondering what Bree planned for the evening. Would his being stuck on a useless phone call change things? Would she leave without him?

4

When Nathan estimated the phone call would take another forty-five minutes, he hadn't truly expected it to last that long. Yet, here he paced, fifty minutes later, waiting on hold for what had to be the tenth time, as the customer service rep finalized his refund. The funds wouldn't actually hit his account for another week, but at least this would get them started heading that way.

A tap at his door had him spinning. He banged his shin and almost tripped over the chair he'd scooted out from the table earlier. Hopping a few times on his uninjured leg, he somehow made it over and flung open the door right as the hold music stopped. Nathan cringed and held up a finger to Bree, who stood in the hallway looking rather lost.

She opened her mouth as if to say something, but he spun around and grabbed a pen, scribbling the confirmation number across the notepad stamped with the hotel logo. Finally, this eternal phone call was over. He assured the rep he didn't need anything else, mentally promising himself he'd never use their company again, and then pushed the *end call* button with relish.

"Sorry about that." Nathan rubbed his leg. "I was almost finished and didn't want to have to go through the whole process again."

"The cruise company?" Bree shifted from foot to foot, barely inside the doorway.

"Yes. Should get my money back next week sometime." He noted her jacket and shoes. "Were you wanting to go somewhere?"

She lifted a shoulder. "Thought I might find a bite to eat."

"Oh. Is it that late already?" A quick glance at his watch confirmed he'd been on the phone even longer than he thought. "Let me grab my shoes."

"I mean, you don't have to. I probably won't go far. Don't even really care what I eat."

"I have the car keys, though." He motioned toward them before thinking. Would she grab them and run off without him? She didn't hate him that much, did she?

"Look, Nathan. I know you said you feel guilty that I'm stuck here, but you really shouldn't. It's sort of my choice, you know." Bree glanced over her shoulder as a family walked down the hallway. "And I know you didn't bargain for being stuck in Dallas during a hurricane."

"We haven't blown away yet." He didn't dare glance through the drapes to see if rain still lashed the windows—no point in depressing himself more. "And it's my choice to stay too."

Her perfectly arched eyebrow lifted higher. "Is it?"

"I wouldn't be here otherwise." He jerked his shoelace so hard it knotted, but he didn't care. He just needed the conversation to end ... or change direction at the least. "Let's go find some dinner."

"Anything you want to eat?" She tugged her jacket closed as he followed her out into the hallway.

He bit back a sigh. Of all their conversations he'd missed over the last month, the back-and-forth to decide where to eat dinner wasn't one. Did it ever end? Or did even married people have this much trouble picking a restaurant?

There had to be an easier way to do this.

The elevator let them out into the lobby, and his gaze landed on the clerk. Hadn't she offered to help them find anything they needed? Well, they needed a place to eat. It was worth a try, anyway.

Bree paused when he didn't turn toward the door, but he had a plan and didn't want to wait long enough to explain.

The clerk pushed her glasses up on top of her head and straightened as he approached the desk. "Good evening. Can I help you?"

"Hi. We were about to head out for dinner, but we didn't have anything particular in mind, and I wondered if you could point us in the direction of something local we could enjoy?"

"I can definitely try." The older woman tapped a pen against the counter. "Were you in the mood for something particular?"

In the middle of shaking his head, he froze. "Got anything that feels New York-ish?"

Bree squeaked beside him, but he couldn't rescind the question now.

The clerk blinked. "New York in Dallas, Texas?"

Nathan shrugged. "Why not?"

The woman pursed her lips and frowned a minute, then straightened with a snap. "Actually, I know just the thing. My daughter was talking about it the other day." She tapped the keys on her computer for a minute before the printer hummed.

Accepting the page from her, he noted the name and address with a smile. "This looks perfect. Thanks so much."

"Enjoy."

Bree tugged at his sleeve as they headed down to the parking garage. "Nathan, wait."

"What's wrong?" He skimmed the line of cars, struggling to remember what their rental looked like.

"New York?"

"Why not? Isn't that where you wish I'd booked a trip?"

Bree huffed. "Does it matter what I wish?"

Nathan pushed the button on the key fob and relaxed as the car in front of them blinked. How had he missed that? He opened her door and motioned her inside.

After a moment's pause, Bree slipped in and started buckling.

"I guess I monopolized your trip, huh? Sorry." Nathan started the car. "I forgot I was supposed to be following your lead this week."

Had he ruined their night before it began?

She shifted as he pulled out into the dreary weather. "It's not that."

It wasn't? What was it then? He didn't consider himself a dunce when it came to reading signs and interpreting body language. And yet, Bree had always had a bit of mystery to her. One of the reasons he'd decided marriage probably wouldn't be a great idea. A decision he needed to remind himself of again instead of slipping so easily into camaraderie with his ex-fiancée.

"I don't know." Bree stared out her window.

"Don't know or won't say?" The GPS spouted another direction, the windshield wipers making it hard to hear.

"I don't care who decides where we eat, Nathan." Bree

flopped her hands in her lap. "I mean, I never made all the decisions for the other road trips I went on, either."

And there was another reminder he needed to back off a little. This wasn't her first trip. And he wasn't the first guy to join her on a vacation, either.

His fingers tightened around the steering wheel.

Bree rolled her eyes as his knuckles whitened. Right. She wasn't supposed to bring up past road trips. It was a subject he'd deemed off-limits despite his challenge for her to show what they'd been like.

But she couldn't exactly explain to him how confusing he was being, either. One minute acting all put-out and guilty that they were still in the city—and with plans to stay, no less. The next moment he was offering up food she might've had if they'd taken her dream honeymoon and opening her car door.

What was she supposed to think?

Before she could come up with anything to say, he parked in front of a place called Grimaldi's. New York-style pizza. Her tastebuds watered at the very thought. Time to take a breath and just soak up the experience on offer here.

The server escorted them to a table halfway across the wood floors. The brick walls might've looked harsh but for the warm glow from the lights above. Friendly chatter echoed through the space, and the smells had her stomach growling.

Bree leaned eagerly over the menu, running her fingers over the words and making noises of approval. "What about this one? It's called the Brooklyn Bridge."

"What's on it?" Nathan's voice held censure. Right. He was pickier about food than she was.

"Roasted red peppers, Italian sausage, and ricotta cheese." Her tummy voiced its approval.

Nathan's lips twisted to the side. "Hmm."

"You liked the peppers in our frittata we made back in college." Her raised eyebrow cut off his protest.

A long sigh escaped him. "Anything else sound good, or is that the one you have your heart set on?"

She rolled her eyes but tapped the top of the menu. "There's a build-your-own option if you're dead set against any of these other yummy sounding pies."

He shook his head. "Get what you want. If there's something on it I don't like, I'll pick it off."

"How old are you?" She couldn't fight back the laugh that bubbled up.

"Old enough to know it's better to keep a girl happy than to worry about some sort of vegetable sneaking onto my pizza." He settled back in his seat with a smirk.

"Hm." For someone supposedly set on keeping her happy, he sure hadn't done a great job of it this last month.

The server appeared, and Bree glanced at Nathan once more before ordering the pizza she'd mentioned and a salad for herself. She knew better than to order something like that for him. Peppers already pushed his limits of adventure.

"I love this place already, and we haven't even tried the food yet." Bree glanced around at the décor.

"Really?" He studied the restaurant again. "What is it about it that makes you love it so much?"

"I think it might be the fact that you tried to find something you knew I'd like." She lifted a shoulder in a half-shrug. "This week isn't going to be anything like either of us planned, but when you asked the hotel clerk for a recommendation, it showed you were at least trying to make the best of the crazy situation."

"You know I don't actually want you to be miserable, right?" A line furrowed between his brows. "That wasn't my intention with anything I've done."

She lined up the salt and pepper shakers in the middle of the table. Could've fooled her. But something told her that asking him why he'd called off the wedding wouldn't get her any answers at this point. Maybe before the end of the week, she could get him to open up and explain things in a way that would make sense.

"Have you thought about finding a place to worship tomorrow?" She leaned back as the server brought out her salad. "Thank you."

"I hadn't made it that far thanks to how long it took with the travel companies." He unwrapped his silverware. "But I'll try and do some research tonight. Text you what time we need to leave."

She nodded as she munched the crunchy greens.

"What did you do on your girl trips?"

"Sure you want me to talk about them?" She couldn't resist the jab at him as she speared another bite of lettuce. "I thought they were off-limits for discussion."

"I told you I wanted to see what it was like. Wanted you to prove to me that ... well, that my imagination was too big for my own good."

Bree wiped her mouth longer than was necessary while she swallowed her bitterness over his lack of trust. "Most of the trips, we tried to be in someone's hometown on a Sunday so we could just worship with their family. This last one, we didn't leave until Monday, so it was a moot point."

"No mid-week Bible study, then?"

"That was the night Skye and Katie got into a huge fight and we all ended up going different directions trying to talk them down." She fiddled with the edge of the tablecloth. "Not our best road trip, although some good came from it."

Their pizza arriving kept him from replying—probably a good thing. He leaned forward and took a big sniff, the corner of his mouth lifting. If nothing else came from this disaster of a former honeymoon, maybe she could at least convince him veggies weren't all bad.

She turned the tray so he could reach the spatula to get the first piece. "Smells good, huh?"

"I suppose you want me to admit you were right?"

"I never say *no* to praise." She winked his way before she could stop herself, an old habit that evidently hadn't died as quickly as their engagement.

He blinked a couple of times and then gave an almost imperceptible shake of his head. "Want to pray?"

When his hands reached for hers, she hesitated only a moment before placing her fingers on his. Warmth swept up her arms and into her chest, and she had to fight back a sob. How could something that felt so right be so wrong?

After clearing his throat, he quickly blessed the food and then tugged his hands free. "Let's eat."

Her choice proved to be a good one. Nathan tucked away three slices and kept eyeing the last few triangles left in the middle of the table. Bree hid her smirk and licked her fingers as she finished off her own second piece. They turned down the offer of dessert and boxed up the last bit to go.

"I've got the check." Nathan waved her away as she offered up some cash.

Didn't that make it more like a date? Was he thinking the same thing? She tucked the money away but mentally promised she'd pay for herself the rest of the time.

Back on the wet streets, they drove slowly to their hotel. At least the rain had softened to a drizzle instead of the earlier downpour, though lightning still brightened the sky every so often. At a corner, a panhandler stood with a sign asking for money for food.

"Roll down your window." Bree pointed to him.

"I'm not giving him money, Bree. We don't know what he'd do with it."

"I want to give him our leftovers." She held up the box.

The older man came up to Nathan's window as the glass lowered. Nathan pushed the box his way. At first the guy hesitated, but then he took it with a nod and a mumbled "Thanks."

"I hope he doesn't just throw it away." Nathan steered them down another block.

"It's not like we wouldn't have ended up doing the same. We're not here long, and that box wouldn't have fit in our minifridges, anyway." Bree smoothed the edge of her shirt. "At least we tried."

Nathan studied her for a moment until a horn behind them reminded him the light had turned green. One more block, and he pulled into the parking garage. Awkwardness settled over her as she climbed out of the car and found her room key in her purse.

The evening could have gone much worse. No. It hadn't been bad at all. Sure, there were some sad moments, but for the most part, it simply reminded her of why she'd loved hanging out with him in the first place. He paused at her door, and she held her breath.

In the past, this would've been where she got a goodnight kiss, but that was before ...

He opened his mouth, then closed it again. He reached as if to pull her in, but then he jerked back. Pressing his lips together, he swallowed so hard his Adam's apple bobbed.

"Thanks for dinner." She kept her voice soft, not wanting to disturb any other guests.

"Sure." He nodded and stepped back. "I'll let you know what I find out about worship services."

"Sounds good." A quick swipe had her door unlocked, and she opened it. "Good night, Nathan."

She stepped inside and leaned against the metal barrier, squeezing her eyes closed and fighting the burning in the back of her throat. Sounds came from the other side of his wall, and she wondered if he regretted the door between them as much as she did. It wasn't supposed to be this way.

Still single.

Still alone every night.

Not even a goodnight kiss anymore.

How would she get any sleep with him so close and still so far away?

5

"Hey. You ready?"

Bree blinked at Nathan before giving a brief nod. She'd forgotten how chipper he was early in the morning. Not that it was that early. Maybe he'd slept better than she had—it wouldn't be hard.

"Let me just grab my purse." She scooped up her small handbag and looped the strap over the shoulder of her simple striped dress. "I didn't think to bring my Bible because the cruise had no mention of services. Though I guess I should've brought it anyway. I just usually do my daily readings on the app."

And now she was babbling. Possibly because she'd already downed three cups of coffee that morning.

"You've been up a while, huh? I heard you talking to someone earlier." Nathan's loafers were silent as they made their way down the carpeted hallway.

"I ... was up anyway, so I grabbed an early morning class to teach." Hopefully her makeup would conceal the tired circles around her eyes. He hadn't mentioned it yet, anyway.

"I guess they're quite a few hours ahead of us over in—where did you say it was?"

"Different countries. Today was India."

"Did you already eat something?" He motioned toward the buffet of cereal, muffins, and bagels.

"A little." She'd discovered long ago that coffee didn't sit well on an empty stomach, so she'd come down before her class to grab a granola bar and a yogurt. "Enough to hold me through to lunch."

He nodded and pulled open the passenger door so she could slide in. "As long as Dallas doesn't have its typical awful traffic on a Sunday morning, it shouldn't take us long to get to the church building. Assuming I read the directions right."

"Sounds good." She fiddled with her purse strap and stared out the window.

Going to worship services shouldn't be this awkward between them. After all, it was one of the first things they'd done together when they started hanging out. It should be one of those things that stayed comfortable regardless. And yet, not a bit of easy conversation came to mind as he maneuvered roads much less crowded than the day before. And he didn't offer anything either—not even a mention of nicer weather.

"This looks like it." He ducked to glance up at the tall steeple as they pulled into the lot. Not many spaces were left near the entrance, so it took him a minute to get the vehicle parked.

She stepped out and joined him at the front of the car.

"Ready?" He crooked his elbow toward her, but she pretended not to see.

"Let's go." She walked across the pavement already warm from the summer sun and smiled at the man greeting inside the door.

"Good morning. Welcome!" The older gentleman handed her a bulletin. "Y'all visiting the area this weekend?"

"Yes, sir." Nathan stuck out his hand. "Nathan Hart. This is my friend, Bree."

Friend. For such a sweet word, it tasted rather bitter.

"We're glad to have you." The man grinned even wider. "I'm afraid you missed our Sunday school classes, but we're just about to get started with worship services. Right through that door."

"Thanks so much." Bree followed Nathan into the auditorium, scanning the room for a space big enough.

"It's our lucky day." Nathan leaned close, his breath tickling the side of her face. "Three rows from the back."

She nodded her agreement and swallowed the emotions he'd stirred in her by being so close. Sliding into the pew, she willed her heart to calm down. No time to analyze anything between her and her ex-fiancé. Worship services would start in less than a minute, according to the countdown on the screen.

"You okay?" Nathan slid in beside her, his long legs bumping hers as he settled.

"Fine." She choked out. *Not fine. Not fine at all, but thanks for asking.*

The song leader saved her from having to field any more concerns. She gladly stood and forced her focus onto the words and notes though the sound of the tenor next to her kept pulling her back to the problem in her mind. How on earth was she supposed to get through the next few days?

Somehow she faked it through the next few songs and communion service, and then the preacher stood behind the pulpit and beamed a smile around the auditorium.

"Welcome! It's a great morning to worship our Lord, is it not?"

Several *amens* sounded around the room.

"We're continuing our study on Ephesians this morning." The minister pulled up a slide on the screen at the front of the room. "Today, we tackle the end of chapter five, and I have to admit to being a bit nervous about it. I tried to convince my wife to stay home, but she insisted on being right here in front of me, where I'll know if I say anything wrong."

Laughter tittered around the room. Nathan opened his Bible and held it between them where she could see it too. His hand ran over the page and when it lifted, she about choked. The section was about wives and husbands. Could God possibly rub more salt in these wounds?

Bree squirmed and steeled herself for whatever might come next in this lesson.

"This part of the Bible gets quite a bad rap nowadays from various groups who don't think a woman should have to submit to her husband. But let's talk about what this is really saying." The preacher moved the slide to the verses and read through them.

"Okay, here's the deal. It does say she should submit to her husband."

Bree couldn't help but glance at Nathan out of the corner of her eye. If their wedding had gone as planned, she would have been expected to follow these verses. Several months ago, she'd been certain none of this would be a problem. That she could follow Nathan anywhere, do anything he asked of her.

But when he'd called things off … she'd begun questioning everything about the last three years. About their relationship. Had any of it been real for him?

Had he decided she wouldn't be the submissive wife these verses required?

The preacher held up his hands as if to hold off any protests. "Now, hold off on complaints for a minute. Because when we look at the next line, we notice the husbands aren't left out, either. They're to love their wives as Christ loved the church. Think about that for a minute."

Nathan moved his arm from the back of the pew and leaned forward, resting his forearms on his thighs. Did this sermon bother him, or was he hearing something he hadn't known before? Did he struggle at all with his decision not to get married?

"How much did Christ love the church?" The preacher cut into her thoughts once more.

Nathan swallowed. And Bree knew why. The answer to that question wasn't an easy one.

"Enough to die for her, right?" The minister prompted. "If a man loves a woman that much, don't you think he'll be treating her so great that she won't have any problems submitting to him? Because he won't want her to do anything she wouldn't be willing to do anyway, right?"

Had Nathan loved her even half that much? Or had those words he said for the last few years simply been words? Because if he'd loved her only a tiny portion of what the Bible said a husband should love a wife, how could he simply end things? How could they be sitting here like this now instead of newlyweds like they were supposed to be?

Bree swallowed a lump of emotion and pinched her lips together in the hopes she wouldn't start crying. This sermon wasn't the kind that normally elicited tears from people, and she didn't want to risk being questioned by strangers.

Nathan shifted again and she drew in a breath. *This is too hard, God!*

"How much did Christ love the church?" The question ran on repeat through Nathan's head for the rest of the sermon. Had he loved Bree that much? Was he able to? Or was it physically impossible for him to actually meet the biblical requirements of a husband?

When they'd gone through pre-marital counseling the year before, he'd been sure of his answers. Sure of their relationship. Their future.

But then he'd gotten that call ...

The reminder.

His jaw clenched and unclenched. He drew in a deep breath through his nostrils, trying to calm his heart rate, not wanting Bree to see how much all this affected him. No. He'd made the right choice no matter what his heart argued every time he caught a whiff of her perfume or her warm arm pressed against his while he shared his Bible.

This was best for both of them.

"In this day and age, marriages are based on a whim, an emotion, a feeling." The preacher shook his head and pounded the podium. "And while it might be a good way to start a rela-tionship, if you don't add trust and respect and even friendship to it, a relationship won't go very far or last through many storms."

See? The preacher was simply backing up Nathan's deci-sion. Nathan nodded.

"But more importantly, if you don't have God as the anchor of your relationship, none of that other stuff will matter at all. Because God is what holds us together when everything else falls apart."

Nathan drew in another breath. Was this torture almost over? Bree squirmed enough to let him know she struggled through this too. Was she regretting being here today ... with him?

After talking about how, as Christians, they were to set the world a better example of what marriage should look like, the preacher wrapped up his lesson, and the congregation stood to sing. Nathan had never been so relieved to be through a sermon in his life. In fact, never before had he been tempted to skip evening services, either. But something about this whole week had him disturbed and confused.

"Hello." The preacher stood at the back of the auditorium and shook hands with everyone as they worked their way out. "I don't think I've met you. Are you visiting this morning?"

"We are. On vacation this week." Nathan reached for Bree and then stopped himself. He no longer had the right to have her at his side when meeting new people, no matter how much his introverted self wished for such help.

"Well, we're glad you found your way to our humble church. Not many couples your age take time out on a vacation to stop for a Bible study." The minister smiled. "Are you enjoying our big city?"

"We're hoping to since the rain stopped." Nathan forced a smile he hoped came across as easy.

"Good, good. And how long have you been married?" A woman who could only be the preacher's wife stepped forward. "I hope this sermon didn't scare you too badly."

"Netta." The preacher's voice was full of affection even as he chided her.

"Stan, you know you tend to be a bit ... forceful in your opinions when you get going." Netta patted his arm. "And these people don't look to have been married long at all."

"We're just friends." Bree finally spoke up. And thank goodness, because Nathan's voice had disappeared.

"Just friends?" Netta looked back and forth between them. "Are you sure? You look so cute together. And Pam said something about you squirming and acting all antsy through that lesson this morning. I guess we just assumed maybe you were newlyweds."

Bree's lips pressed together as she cut him a side glance.

He swallowed a lump of emotion. "No, ma'am."

"Of course, how silly of me." Netta flapped her hands. "People don't honeymoon in Dallas."

Nathan bit back a chuckle. Almost a honeymoon. But he wasn't about to let Netta know a hint of that, either.

"Well, what all do you have planned?" Stan glanced between the two of them.

"We honestly haven't had much of a chance to plan it out. We ended up here sort of on accident thanks to the hurricane going through." Bree shrugged. "I hope to research some ideas this afternoon."

"Well, you have to eat lunch, right?" Netta raised an eyebrow. "The best place to go on a Sunday afternoon is the farmer's market. It's like a smorgasbord of different foods to taste."

"Isn't that, like, fresh vegetables and stuff that's not cooked yet?" Nathan frowned. He didn't mind a few veggies here and there, but he was more of a meat and potatoes kind of guy.

"Oh, honey. Not the one in Dallas. It has that, too, but there's also amazing food; homemade, crafty items; and live music." She waved her hands at them again. "Go. Put on something comfy and experience one of the best hidden treasures in Dallas. And I hope we'll see you again this evening. We can give you more ideas."

"That all sounds amazing." Bree's voice was more cheerful than it had been all morning.

Stan chuckled. "Sounds like you have your marching orders."

"I guess so." Nathan rubbed the back of his neck. "Thanks for the suggestion."

"We'll see you tonight." Netta pointed a finger at him as he started them toward the door.

He didn't answer out loud, but part of him wondered if she might come hunt him down if he didn't have them back for evening services. Bree walked quietly beside him across the parking lot and slid into the car. He quickly cranked the air conditioner and then followed the instructions the GPS spouted to get them back to the hotel.

"We don't have to do the farmer's market if you don't want to. I know it's not really your kind of thing." Bree's voice was soft, and she didn't look his way when she said it.

"No. It's fine." He tapped the steering wheel. "After all, as Mrs. Netta pointed out, we have to eat lunch somewhere. And it sounds like something you'd enjoy. You're the trip guru, right?"

Bree cringed, and he knew he hadn't kept the sarcasm out of his voice as much as he'd intended. Yet another reason it was good they wouldn't be together any more after this week. He just had to get through the next few days, and then he could let her move on without him—no longer have to worry about hurting her again.

"So, you want to go change?" He asked the question if only to break the heavy silence that had taken up residence in the tiny car after his last words.

"At least grab some more comfortable shoes, if that's okay."

"Of course."

More awkward silence. The message of the sermon, the way they were mistaken for newlyweds, the embarrassment of the whole situation—it all settled in the already thick air and made it almost impossible to breathe. He was more than grateful to be able to park in the shaded parking garage a few minutes later.

"Guess I'll see you again in a few minutes." He paused outside her door.

"Okay." Still, she didn't look his way. "Or I could go by myself if you'd rather stay here and nap or something."

"Bree, it's fine. I can ... eat vegetables two days in a row." Though he didn't have to like it.

A giggle burst from her, and she slapped a hand over her mouth as if she hadn't meant for it to happen.

"Yeah, yeah. Thanks a bunch." He rolled his eyes but grinned. "See you in a few minutes."

Inside his hotel room, or what he'd started mentally calling the torture chamber, he listened to the sounds of her rustling around on the other side of that awful connecting door. Quickly he stepped to the sink and flipped the faucet on—the running water helped block out the noises bringing to mind all sorts of images he wasn't allowed to dream about now. His own fault.

But a right decision was a right decision, no matter how painful it might be. And he wouldn't change his mind.

6

"Whoa." Nathan slowed the car to a crawl in front of the Dallas Farmer's Market.

A red tractor stood sentinel before the two large structures, one open air, labeled "The Shed," and a second closed in with "The Market." He jerked to attention as someone honked behind them and sped up a bit to follow the signs for parking. Behind the market was a garage, over half-full, from the looks of things.

"When she said farmer's market, I pictured something more like what we have at home in Kentucky." Bree's voice held awe.

"Small, pop-up tent things with locally grown tomatoes and honey, right?" He inched into a spot and turned the car off.

"Right." Bree shook her head and got out, her bright pink capris standing out beneath her sleeveless chambray top. "This is amazing. I'm so glad Mrs. Netta suggested it. Let's go."

"Oh man." Nathan locked the vehicle and then spun around to try and keep up. "I'm in for it now, aren't I?"

This was right up Bree's alley. She was one of those people

who could find amazing food in the most podunk, lackluster places. This would knock her socks off.

Acoustic guitar and something else sent notes their way as they rounded the corner and mingled with a crowd of other people who had the same idea. Three men stood at the entrance to the market side, crooning about how much they loved Texas. Nathan barely kept from rolling his eyes. Talk about a stereotype.

"So, where do we start?" Nathan glanced between the two buildings but couldn't discern any rhyme or reason.

"Those people came out with food." Bree pointed to a group walking out of the Market building. "Let's go that way."

"Food sounds ... good." At least it usually did. Nathan was wary of what might be available here, though.

Various aromas hit them as they stepped into the blissfully air-conditioned structure. Around the concrete floor, restaurants and food stands offered a much larger variety than he'd expected. It was like an upscale food court.

"Barbecue, Vietnamese, fish, tacos, or ooh—Cajun." Bree pointed at each place as she mentioned them. "If you really want an idea of what my last trip was like, we could eat there."

More salt in the wound. What was that? The fifth time she'd brought that up in the last two days? Seventh?

Bree caught the look on his face and scanned the area again. "Right. Hmm. Oh. Look at that glorious cheese!"

He followed her toward a booth that did indeed have a glass case full of various rounds of his favorite dairy product. He was actually the one who'd finally convinced Bree there was more to life than plain old American, cheddar, or mozzarella. How someone with a name spelled almost like one of his favorite soft cheeses hadn't known about it, he still couldn't understand.

"Mm." Bree's nose practically smushed against the glass.

"Would you like a sample?" The lady behind the counter offered a warm smile and a bite of Gruyère.

"She's speaking our language." Bree laughed and then closed her eyes as she munched the nibble. "This is so good, Nathan. Seriously. Try a bite."

His heart warred within him as the Bree he'd fallen in love with three years ago stood before him in all her glory.

Bree's giggle was the first thing that attracted Nathan to her. She'd been sitting with friends in the Commons, and her laughter bounced over to the swing where he'd been trying to study. But there was no concentrating on Statistics with her joy distracting him over and over again. He ended up staring at her instead of the papers full of numbers in his lap. And when her baby blues looked over his way, he might as well have been struck by lightning.

Not that he got up the nerve to go meet her then. Oh, no. Instead, he simply sought her out at each event and then let his eyes follow her movements and cheerfulness from across the room.

She'd made first contact. "Hi."

It only took a minute to look down and tie his shoe, and the next thing he knew, she stood right in front of him, her hand out to shake.

"Hi." The word had come out on a breath, barely audible.

"I'm Bree Henley."

"Nathan." His name squeaked by his lips, but only just.

She tilted her head to the side with a little grin. "Well, Nathan. It's nice to meet you."

And then, she'd reached over and clasped his hand where he hadn't gotten around to shaking hers yet. That was all it took. He was hooked, all in, and done. And when she hadn't made it over to speak to him first at the next event, he made sure to look for her and move his feet instead of just his eyes.

"Earth to Nathan." Bree waved her hand in his face in the here and now, bringing him back from easier days. "Ready to move on and find something more substantial?"

"Sure." He hooked his thumb over his shoulder. "Should we try the barbecue?"

"I'm game if you are."

"Remember how Mike Kowitz used to boast that Texas had the best? Now we finally get to find out." He studied the menu, not sure how much to order.

"I'd totally forgotten about him. Didn't he graduate the year before us?" She pointed to several things. "Maybe we should get the sampler plate and split it? Then we can still nibble at other places too. There's an ice cream spot over there that looks delicious."

"Okay." After years of dating, he knew better than to argue when she made a food suggestion. She was almost always right, even if he didn't like to admit it.

After trying four different kinds of smoked meat—though none of them were the pork he was used to—they meandered a bit more. Bree talked him into trying a new flavor of ice cream, snitching a bite of her own before he could get in his first lick. And not looking the least bit guilty.

Then she purchased a large bag of popcorn flavored with some spice he'd never heard of. When she held the bag his way, he hesitated a moment before accepting. Trying different meats and cheeses was one thing, but new spices? One lift of her perfectly curved brow, and he tucked back a groan before grabbing several kernels and tossing them in his mouth. A bit earthy, with just a bit of kick to it. But not bad.

"Right?" Bree's mouth twisted in a smirk. "Let's go wander through the area next door. I'm excited to see what all is there. Maybe I can find something for my dad for his birthday next month. Isn't your mom's birthday soon too?"

He swallowed a lump of guilt—his mom's birthday hadn't even crossed his mental radar. "In a few weeks. You remember my mom's birthday?"

Bree looked him straight in the eye. "She was almost my mom too."

An arrow couldn't have pierced his heart any deeper.

"You can browse for something for her too." Bree turned on her heel and moved forward once more.

He followed her back out into the heat, winding around strollers and various groups standing around listening to the music. Flowers, bags of produce, and even garden sculptures filled the arms of people walking out—no telling what he might find here.

Bree flitted like a bee from stall to stall, touching a necklace or pair of earrings, giggling over funny signs, holding up a flowy blouse before putting it back after a glance at the price tag. As she chatted with a honey vendor about beekeeping and the health benefits of the various shades in the jars, he marveled once more at her ease in talking to people she'd just met. It was a skill he'd never perfected.

Honestly, it was one of the reasons he'd considered them perfect for each other. Her extroverted tendencies and love of adventure had offset his more tentative nature. He'd kept her from going too crazy, and she'd added zest to his otherwise boring life. But simply having someone to keep him from being humdrum wasn't a good enough reason to continue ... or restart ... a relationship, no matter how much he loved watching her in her element.

"Oh, look." Bree held up a hand-carved Christmas ornament featuring a cutout of the Dallas skyline. "I love grabbing an ornament or something from each place I visit. And this one is lovely. What do you think?"

"What did you get from your last trip?" He didn't meet her eyes as he asked the question.

She nodded to the vendor that she wanted to buy the find though it was a bit more expensive than she'd normally pay. "An ornament with Stone Mountain on it. That's where Katie and I spent the last day together."

"No one else?"

"Nope. Skye chose to run off to Six Flags that day." Bree pointed ahead. "Let's go look over there. I bet your mom would like something from that table."

The booth was filled with items painted with bluebonnets. Thimbles, towels, mugs, keychains. Even old cans and bottles repurposed as vases and pencil holders. She held up a thimble.

"Your mom sews, right?"

"Yes." He studied the tiny porcelain piece. "You're right. She'd probably love adding this to her collection."

Bree swallowed back her satisfaction. No need to rub it in. She'd just relish being able to share her love of finding the perfect gift.

"I'm going over there for a minute. See if anything catches my eye for Dad."

"Sure." He paid the lady behind the bluebonnet table.

Despite being in an area filled with other people, the close proximity to Nathan was beginning to get to her. This all reminded her too much of times in the past when they'd dated. And he obviously didn't want to go down that road any further, or he wouldn't have called off their wedding.

So, why was he so insistent on being here now?

"Evening services start at five." Nathan appeared at her elbow as she picked up a hand-carved pocketknife. "Anything else you want to see before we head back to the hotel? I'd love to cool off just a bit before we return to the church building."

"No. I think I'm good." Bree followed his lead back past the music and through the sunshine to the parking garage. "I guess Mrs. Netta didn't scare you off this morning?"

"I think I'm more scared of not showing up because of her."

Bree laughed and slid into the car. "I get that."

It didn't take long to return to their downtown hotel, but there were only about forty-five minutes left before they'd need to leave. Bree washed her face and checked a few emails. A quick brush of her hair and a dab of make-up and she was ready. But she had no idea how long Nathan would take.

A knock on her door kept her from wondering what to do next.

Once again, they found a seat near the back of the church building and settled in for a sermon. This time it wasn't on marriage. It was on trust.

Not much better, all things considered.

Netta greeted them warmly after services, squeezing Bree's hands between her own. "Did you have a good afternoon? How was the market?"

"It was amazing. Thank you so much for the suggestion." Bree had loved this woman instantly and was almost sad they wouldn't know her longer than today.

"Now, what do you have planned for the rest of your time here?"

"We haven't actually discussed it yet."

"Good." Netta turned and waved down a few other gentlemen across the foyer. "Gerald! Ralph! Come here, please."

Before Bree knew it, she was in a deep discussion of the best places to hit in Dallas.

"Of course, you could drive over to Fort Worth to see the

cattle yards." Ralph drawled, his thumbs hooked in his pockets.

"These kids don't have any interest in cattle." Gerald shook his head, his jowls wiggling. "They'd probably enjoy those gondola things my Missie's always talking about. Said they're so romantic."

"Gondolas. Huh. Nothing Texas about gondolas. Aren't they from some shmancy country across the ocean?" Ralph rolled his eyes. "They need something that says *Texas*. Oh. How about the Sixth Floor Museum? It's where Kennedy got himself killed. Can't miss that."

Bree blinked. And Nathan wore a dazed expression as well.

"Or there's the Arboretum. Should be all bloomed out right about now." Gerald nodded and brushed his combover down. "My Missy always likes to take the grandkids there."

"What about the carriage rides, then?" A woman hopped into the conversation and elbowed Gerald. "That's something romantic to do. I think they're still offering those."

"My grandkids are forever talking about that park—the one with the bridge and stuff." Ralph snapped his fingers. "What's it called?"

"Clyde Warren?"

"Yeah, that's it." Ralph nodded. "Should be some things to do there."

"That's a lot of ideas. Thanks so much." Bree broke in before they could mention anything else. If they kept going, they'd come up with more than she and Nathan had time to accomplish.

"You should definitely do the Sixth Floor Museum, though." Gerald shook his finger at them. "American history at its finest."

"Yes, sir." Bree nodded and took a step back, tugging Nathan's sleeve to encourage him to do the same. "We'll definitely consider these ideas this evening. It was great meeting you all."

Somehow, they managed to escape the church building after only having to accept five more suggestions and three more handshakes. Bree wiped a hand across her forehead and laughed.

"Whew. Texans sure are friendly."

Nathan chuckled, a sound she hadn't heard in a while. "Seem to be."

"How about finding a bite to eat, and then we can look up some of those ideas we got?"

"Sure."

After settling in at a sandwich place, Bree pulled out a small notepad and some paper, then did a search for the best things to do in Dallas. At the top of most of the lists was the museum they'd mentioned. Apparently, they weren't the only ones who deemed it a must-see.

"Looks like that museum is a big deal." She took a bite of her BLT and scribbled it down. "Here's the park they mentioned. And the cattle yard."

Nathan snorted across the table. "You really want to go see cows?"

"Nope. Just reading off ideas."

He smirked and munched a potato chip.

"Here's a post about all the graffiti art in Deep Ellum, which is an area near here. Or dinner in Reunion Tower, which gives an amazing view of Dallas. There's a zoo, a baseball stadium, and Six Flags." Bree wrinkled her nose and shook her head. "I have less than no desire to do baseball or Six Flags. Those were ruined on the last trip."

"They were?" Nathan's brows furrowed.

"I told you about Skye sneaking off to Six Flags, right? After we did the baseball game. Anyway, it ruined the end of our trip. Let's do something else."

"Maybe start with the museum and go from there?"

"Sounds like a plan." Bree slurped her lemonade. "How do you feel about flowers?"

"Flowers?"

"The Arboretum does look like fun."

"Flowers." Nathan sighed. "I supposed if this were one of your girls' trips, you'd go see flowers."

Bree leaned back and tapped her chin. "I don't know. I mean, Skye might not find much interest in it. But this trip is so different from any of the trips I took with Katie and Skye that it's hard to compare anyway. Every place has a different feel, different things to see. And when you travel with different people, it changes a trip too."

"So, your last girls' trip wasn't like the first ones because you added in those guys?" Nathan's brow wrinkled, and he wadded up his food wrapper.

Bree breathed in through her nostrils, trying to control her anger. How many more times would she have to defend herself?

"None of our trips were the same." Her voice was laced with steel. "But no. The last one was different too. I think we all knew it would probably be our last since I was supposed to be getting married and Katie was starting a new job."

A solemnity settled over the table and Nathan shifted in his seat. "Guess we better head back to the hotel."

She nodded. "Busy day tomorrow."

Twenty-four hours of wondering about the man accompanying her. Was he really as hurt and angry as he acted? Or was something else going on? Because she could've sworn she saw the guy she fell in love with several times today. Why was Nathan hiding him?

7

Bree fidgeted with her purse strap, trying to control the urge to yell at Nathan. He only took three wrong turns before finding a parking garage he considered reasonably priced. He shot her a grin after turning off the car and blinked at what must've been a scowl on her face. She just rolled her eyes.

Was it worth all that to save two dollars?

They walked side by side the few blocks toward the Grassy Knoll. It was labeled with a large banner in case you couldn't figure out what it was by looking. Today the sun shone down on families playing in shady spots as they waited for their turn to go through the museum.

"It doesn't look like a museum, does it?" Bree studied the old warehouse. "If it weren't for the signs, I probably would've passed right by this place and never known the historical importance."

"It's not like it was a museum before the history happened here." Nathan held the door for her to go in before him. "I'm sure it was chosen because it was rather nondescript."

Made sense to her.

"It costs how much?" Nathan asked the clerk to repeat the price. "And that doesn't include the headphones to listen to all the information about what went on?"

"Seriously." Bree slapped her debit card on the counter. "Two please. With headphones."

"Bree!" Nathan hissed, but she ignored him.

"Thank you so much." Bree flashed a grin at the cashier, who gave them both a wary look. She grabbed the headphones and marched toward the elevators.

"Bree, wait." Nathan tugged on her sleeve. "Why did you do that?"

"Because you were gearing up to try and haggle. This isn't a place you can talk the price down just because you think it's higher than it needs to be. It's a museum. Sometimes you just have to accept that things cost more than you want to pay."

"We could've gone and done something else. Or gone through without the headphones."

"But the headphones are what tells us about all the different photos and artifacts. We wouldn't have gotten as much out of it without them." Bree shook her head and then pushed one set of headphones into his chest. "Why does it always have to be about money with you?"

"I'm an accountant. Money is my job."

Bree spun on her heel and pushed the button for the elevators. "In case you haven't noticed, you're not working right now."

"All the more reason to not spend more money than I should."

"Well, now you don't have to worry about it. Because I paid for it." She stepped inside the elevator and crossed her arms.

Nathan remained outside, his mouth agape, until the doors started to close again. He forced his arm through at the last moment and followed her inside, shooting looks of apology to the others waiting. They rode silently to the sixth floor.

Stepping out at the beginning of the tour, all around them were silent or talking only in whispers, in reverence of what happened here. The shot had come from this level and killed John F. Kennedy. Bree followed the prompts in her ears, learning about Kennedy, his family, his presidency, and why he'd been in town that particular day.

By the end, she wiped tears from her cheeks.

It was their turn to look through the window where the shot had happened. "It was here. I am standing at the same place as whoever killed the president stood."

"So, you don't believe the Lee Harvey Oswald story?" He leaned forward to stare down into the plaza where the car had been.

"It's hard to know what to believe after reading all that." She motioned back toward the exhibits they'd already seen.

He tilted his head, held his hands up to frame where the car had passed. Pushed his fingers closer to each other and tilted his head. "It wasn't an impossible shot, but it wouldn't have been easy either. Maybe why it took two bullets?"

"What are you doing?" Bree yanked his hands down and looked around, hoping no one overheard him.

"I was wondering exactly what angle it was and how he figured out velocity and everything. I mean, this is Texas, so there was probably wind. And he couldn't have known the speed the car would have been driving. But he would have had to take all that into consideration to figure out exactly when to fire and where to aim. And it got me curious about the numbers."

"Math doesn't stop for you, does it?" She kept her voice low though she wanted to yell and scream. "This is a murder we're talking about."

"I know that. I'm not trying to be mean or anything. I was just curious."

"People's lives were taken—ruined—it was real life. Jackie Kennedy lost her husband just like that." Bree snapped. "And you're standing here wondering about the angle and velocity?"

Bree shook her head and stomped off, whacking the elevator button once more. Too much. Nathan was too much today. First with the insistence on finding cheaper parking, then wanting to skimp on the entrance fee, and now taking a tragedy and summing it all up with cold, hard numbers.

Well, he could keep his numbers. Maybe he was right after all. Maybe they weren't good together. Because she couldn't just read about real people who lived through such an awful event—not to mention the one who didn't—without empathizing at least a little. And she couldn't stand to be around someone so emotionally detached when she was so moved.

She returned her headphones, nodded at the security guard, and headed toward the exit. Out into the sunlight she stormed, looking both ways and then crossing to the memorial on the other side of the Grassy Knoll. She sniffled as she studied the words etched in the stone.

"What did I do wrong?" Nathan took a tentative step near Bree, where she'd stopped across the street.

"Really? You really don't know?" Her voice was somewhere between angry and sad.

"Pretend like I can't read your mind and tell me." Because it would've been too easy for God to give man that ability!

"You took a tragic event and whittled it down to numbers. Made it clerical and cold and unfeeling." With each modifier, she sliced her hand through the air, coming closer to his chest than he was comfortable with.

"Bree, I'm sorry I tend to think about things in mathematical terms. That's who I am, and I thought you knew that after all these years. But I wasn't trying to make the event seem less than it was. I know it rocked the whole nation when it happened. But we are rather removed from it. I mean, we weren't even a glimmer in our parents' eyes when it went down."

"That doesn't mean we can't feel the grief. That we can't go back and learn from it and use the empathy as we go forward."

"I'm not sure what you mean."

Bree huffed and glanced upward as if looking for inspiration from the sky. "Jackie Kennedy lost the man she loved that day. Sure, their marriage wasn't perfect, but that doesn't mean her heart didn't rip out of her chest the moment that bullet hit his head."

Nathan had no reply to that. It was the truth, but he didn't see why it had Bree so upset.

"Obviously, I've never lost a husband." Bree's voice choked on the last word, and she swallowed before she could continue. "But I can imagine how awful it was for her to sit beside her husband while he bled in her arms and nothing she could do would save him. I can imagine what it's like to lose someone you wanted to spend the rest of your life with and have that dream and promise ripped out of your arms forever."

Nathan's heart skipped a beat. Was Bree still talking about the Kennedys, or had this gotten a lot more personal? Is that how she viewed his calling off their engagement? As a dream ripped out of her hands?

Dashing at her eyes, Bree moved on to look at another plaque farther away. He stayed where he was, hoping if she had some space, she could calm herself down. This was too awkward. A museum wasn't supposed to make things so emotional.

Didn't this simply confirm what he'd been saying for a month now? He couldn't even get through a museum without ticking this woman off. How on earth would they have been able to do forever?

As much as he couldn't understand her outburst and frustration, though, he longed to wrap his arms around her and give her whatever comfort she'd find there. Would she still find solace snuggled against his chest? Several times at school, he'd held her while she cried over some injustice or another. But that was back before he realized she deserved better than him.

He stepped to her side and gently placed a hand on her back. "Hey."

"Oh." Bree spun and burrowed her head into his chest, her arms going around his waist just like they'd done a million times. But that had been before ...

He stood frozen for a moment. This hadn't been what he'd been going for when he reached out, and yet it was okay. More than okay, if he were being truthful. Softly he rubbed her back until Bree's muffled sobs subsided. He started to ask if it was really as bad as all that but then remembered he was part of the reason she was crying. Might not be the best idea.

The tears went on longer than he expected. As awkward as it was to hold a crying woman in a public square, it also felt righter than anything he'd done in a long while. Since graduating over a month before. Since he'd called off their wedding.

"I made your shirt all soggy." Bree hiccuped and rubbed at the wet spot on his front.

The warmth of her hand through the damp material had his heart doing things it wasn't supposed to. He took one step back. Time to distract.

"We're going to the Arboretum this afternoon, right?" He

shrugged. "It'll dry eventually. Want to find somewhere to eat?"

Bree nodded, a few of her hairs clinging to his chin.

He brushed them away, his fingers enjoying the silky feel more than they should. *Off limits, bud. Remember your reasons. Stick to your guns.*

"What sounds good to you?" Maybe if he got her talking food, he could get his own emotions back under control too.

Bree whipped out her phone and scrolled through an app that showed various eateries in the area. "Rather than try to find something where we'd have to move the car, let's see what's close. Sound good?"

"Sure. Not moving the car sounds great."

"Tacos, pasta, burgers. Ooh!" Bree held up her phone to show a restaurant. "Chinese. Only a couple blocks away."

Nathan couldn't help but wrinkle his nose. "No. Gonna put my foot down on that one."

"But Chinese is so good."

"Agree to disagree." Nathan shook his head. "You've already got me agreeing to spend my afternoon looking at flowers. I don't feel it's fair for you to insist on this too."

"Have you ever tried Chinese?" Bree propped a fist on her hip, and even though her face was still a bit splotchy from her earlier tears, his pulse picked up a notch at the picture she made.

"That's beside the point."

"It's not." She poked a finger at him. "You said you wanted to see what it's like to tag along on my girls' trips. Well, mister, this is it. We try new things. We have new experiences. We expand our horizons."

"And museums and flowers aren't enough new things for one day?" He narrowed his eyes. "Especially when yesterday I did the whole farmer's market thing too?"

"Nope. It's as many as we can cram in the time we're on the trip. Let's go." She walked to the corner and pushed the button to cross the street.

He rushed to catch up again. "Bree, seriously. Don't we get to vote or something?"

"There's only two of us. How would that work?"

"Rock, paper, scissors?"

She paused on the sidewalk and held out a fist. "Ready, set, go!"

Before he could even think straight, she was banging her fist up and down. He threw out a flat hand, but hers was out with two fingers straightened, like scissors. He lost anyway.

"No fair. I didn't have time to get ready."

"Please." Bree flipped her hair back and rolled her eyes. "You always choose paper."

"What?" He blinked as he speed walked to keep up with her. She was right, but even he hadn't realized he went with the same one more than seventy-five percent of the time. Did she actually know him better than he did? And did that mean she knew everything ...?

"There it is." Bree pointed to a little spot advertising a buffet and egg rolls.

"I'm not going to find anything that sounds good." Nathan groaned.

"I'll help. I haven't steered you wrong food-wise yet." Bree tossed a grin over her shoulder and entered the building. "Come on."

Reluctantly he forked out enough money to cover both their lunches. As they grabbed a plate and moved down the counter, Bree talked him into trying a few types of chicken and some rice. He drew the line at the veggies. A man had his limits.

"Egg roll?" Bree held one up with tongs.

"What's in those things, exactly?"

"I'm not sure." She studied it with head tilted before plopping it on her plate next to several other unidentifiable piles of food. "But they're good."

"Pass. Thanks."

At the table, Bree grinned at him. "You're going to fall in love with Chinese. Which one will you try first?"

"Um. Let's say a prayer first." Anything to delay the inevitable.

As soon as the *amen* was over, Bree dug in, winking at him. "Go ahead then."

He released a slow stream of air through his lips, sent up another silent prayer that he could at least get enough down to have energy for the afternoon, and took a bite. Not bad, but not something he'd want again either. Bree raised an eyebrow, and he shrugged in response.

Seemed that was enough for her. She took another bite and paused. This time, no happy expression followed. Instead, she chewed slowly, contemplating something. Hopefully not anything that had to do with him trying yet another type of food for dinner. Maybe he could find a place that served mashed potatoes or mac n' cheese. They had those in Dallas, didn't they?

Whatever had caused the expression quickly passed, and Bree ate as if she'd never made that face. Though he noticed when she was done that she hadn't eaten as much of one of the piles of food as she had the others. Strangely enough, it was the one with broccoli and carrots—two of her favorite things.

"You get your craving settled?" Nathan pushed his plate away, only a few bites left. At least he'd gotten his money's worth down his throat.

"Yeah. Not the best I've ever had, but it was okay for now. I can get better when I'm back in Memphis with Katie."

"Ready to go then?"

"Yep. To the Arboretum." Bree slung her purse over her shoulder and followed him back out into the heat.

If they'd been smart, they'd have done the outside activities in the morning when the heat wasn't at its peak, but they hadn't considered the weather when planning today's activities. Maybe there'd be enough shade to cool things down, at least a little. If not, he might encourage more speed walking.

8

"So, not only do I have to pay for more parking, but we have to pay to walk through these gardens too?" Nathan couldn't help but grumble as he stopped the car. From what he'd seen so far, he couldn't fathom why Bree loved trips like this so much.

"I'll handle the parking cost since this was my idea." Bree didn't wait for him to come around and open her door. "If you don't want to walk through these lovely gardens, stay here in the car. But it would probably be cooler under all those shade trees."

"More than likely be even cooler in an air-conditioned building." He muttered as he followed her to the entrance.

Bree finished paying for herself and accepted the map of the gardens with a smile. The clerk motioned him forward, and he sighed but shelled out another entrance fee. So much for this trip being cheaper than anything they'd originally considered doing this week. Though he shouldn't complain too much since Bree had paid for his museum tour that morning. Did that make them even or put her ahead after dinner two nights before?

"You coming?" Bree glanced over her shoulder and motioned him on. "I think we're going to see beauty no matter which direction we pick. Do you care?"

The dappled sunlight coming through the trees sent a glow about Bree that tightened his chest. Beauty indeed. Though he couldn't admit to feeling that way. Especially since he'd been the one to sever their connection.

"Nathan?" Her question reminded him he hadn't replied.

"You pick."

They meandered from garden to garden, Bree stopping to exclaim over flowers she wasn't familiar with or remark about a particular scent of one or another. The trial garden, where various plants not native to Texas grew, kept her attention for quite a while.

"Where do you think they originally came from? If they're not from here, how do they survive here for longer than a season?" Bree fingered a purple blossom.

Nathan shrugged. "I know even less about flowers than you do."

Pink flowers framed a walkway in another section, the branches arching to meet in the middle overhead.

"Wow. I don't think I've ever seen crepe myrtles so tall." Bree tilted her head back and spread her arms as if to soak it all in.

Gorgeous.

Nathan swallowed and cleared his throat. "Yep. They're tall."

"Oh, look at these." Bree leaned over to sniff some blossoms half an hour later.

"What are they? Roses?" Nathan tilted his head as he studied one. Didn't look like any rose he'd ever seen before, but he didn't make it a habit to study flora and fauna like a lot of girls did.

"Camellias." Bree fingered one of the petals. "Aren't they lovely?"

"Sure." He used his map as a fan to try and move some of the hot air around a bit.

"Roses are this way." Bree pointed and then marched them further down the path. "See the difference?"

This garden was full of various colors and shades of roses —some big, some tinier than he knew existed. Without seeing the flowers side by side, he still couldn't have told her what made them different, but she wasn't waiting for him to answer anyway. Instead, she'd moved on toward what looked like a gazebo-shaped structure, all metalwork.

"Makes me think of the scene in *The Sound of Music* where the girl sings about being sixteen but about to turn seventeen." Bree grinned as she stepped inside and started humming. "I always thought it would be fun to act that scene out."

"You're not sixteen, you know."

"Yes, I know." Bree rolled her eyes but twirled around the circumference. "But it was always romantic how they danced their way around, him helping her jump from bench to bench while the rain pounded outside."

"Doesn't sound safe to me." Nathan stepped inside, too, though he couldn't picture the same thing she had in her head.

"And then, at the end, a kiss!" Bree swept around, faster now, before almost running into him where he stood in the entrance. Her palms landed on his shoulders, her chest heaving from her dance.

His hands caught her elbows. Those blue eyes of hers widened. They kept ending up like this. Where both got lost in the moment and forgot the reality of their situation.

Instead, the past crept in and fogged up the edges, layering memories over the here and now until it was hard to remember which they were supposed to be living. And, for a moment, no one else existed in the world but the two of them, in the middle of this immense garden, in the metal gazebo, man and woman.

As if they had a mind of their own, his feet moved a step closer. Bree licked her lips, her gaze searching his. Nathan leaned even closer, caught up in the scene, as if her words earlier had dictated what should happen.

"Mama! Look!" A little voice nearby jerked Nathan back to reality.

He wasn't supposed to be this close to Bree. Definitely shouldn't be a breath away from kissing her. He stepped back and dropped his hands.

"I think we're getting closer to the lake now." He turned and looked around as if the water would jump up and show itself through the bushes and trees. "Want to see if we can find it?"

Bree frowned, pressed her lips together, wrapped her arms around her middle. "Sure."

They walked quietly for a few minutes, each on an opposite side of the path. Bree's attention stayed fixed anywhere but on him. And he was okay with that. Or at least, he was working to be okay with it.

"Oh." Bree let out a breath.

Ahead, sunlight sparkled off a reflecting pool, still and calm. On the other side, small waves rippled across the lake stretched out to the horizon. Bree stepped right up to the edge of the pond and breathed deeply. What was she thinking?

There had been a time not so long ago when he would've been able to read her more easily than any of the science fiction books he loved. Or at least better than any other human around. But this trip, she had a wall up, and it was the most unnatural thing in the world for someone as open and caring and kind as Bree.

And he found he missed being able to see her expression and know what kind of mood she was in.

After a few more moments, Bree turned and motioned down the path again. "Wander a bit more?"

"Might as well get our money's worth." He followed her lead though the interrupted moment from earlier haunted him. Would he have completed what he started if that other family hadn't shown up? And what would that have done to the rest of their week together?

Best to push it aside and leave it as it was—unfinished.

Bree paused at a pond and watched the koi swimming around under lily pads. A smile twitched the edges of her lips up, and some of the unease inside Nathan relaxed. This really was a peaceful place to spend the afternoon despite the crazy heat.

As Bree moved on, she rubbed her belly, a tiny crease forming between her eyes. But as quickly as he noticed it, it passed, and she skipped ahead to a low waterfall. Had he actually seen something wrong, or were his eyes playing tricks?

He'd keep an eye on her, no matter what. Even though she'd always claimed he was the more stubborn of the two, he knew she could give him his money's worth in willpower. And after him making such a big deal about lunch, if that was what caused her problems, she'd probably rather die than admit it.

***

"Look at all the colors." Bree massaged her stomach once more as it let out a loud gurgle. Maybe her words had covered up the noise.

Nathan shot her a sideways glance but didn't comment. "Yep. Lots of colors."

This wasn't working. Bree swallowed a lump of nausea and sent up a prayer. *Please, God, let it just be that I'm overheated and not ... a virus ... or something I ate.*

Of all the lousy rotten stupid things to happen on a trip, food poisoning was at the tip top of her list. She should've known better than to take more than one bite of that foul-tasting dish at lunch, but Nathan had watched her so closely. And she'd made such a big deal out of Chinese being good.

Pride went before a fall. Or, in this case, a miserable afternoon.

Her tummy protested once more, and she breathed in through her nose and out through her mouth, trying to will away the increasing queasiness. None of her begging and pleading ... or anything else ... helped, though. The later the afternoon grew, the worse her belly rumbled and churned.

Spying a bench, Bree sank onto it, hopeful that sitting would alleviate a bit of her discomfort.

"You okay?" Nathan propped a foot on the bench next to her and leaned his elbows on his knee. "You don't look so great."

"Just what every girl wants to hear." Bree forced the words through her semi-clenched lips. If she opened her mouth too wide, she feared more than words would spew through.

"Bree, seriously." Nathan cocked his head to the side as he studied her. "You look rather white. Almost green."

"I think I maybe overheated or something." Fanning herself with the map, Bree offered a smile that might or might not have looked more like a cringe. "We probably aren't drinking enough water out in this heat."

"You think you're getting dehydrated?" Nathan straightened and looked around. "I saw a little restaurant back that way. I'll go get some water."

"No, don't." She wasn't sure why she protested. If he went to get the water, at least she could formulate a plan in peace as to the best way to handle what seemed more and more imminent.

"Why not? If you're feeling bad, it's sometimes a sign of dehydration or even early signs of a heat stroke. My brother used to work as a counselor at summer camp and always ordered us to drink more water when he came home." Nathan snickered. "Though one time I filled up my water bottle only to start a water fight with him for being so bossy. The younger brother should never try bossing the older."

"Mm." It was all Bree could manage. A storm brewed in her midsection, and she wasn't sure how much longer until it broke free.

"I'm going to get water. You stay right here." Nathan hopped up again. "Don't move."

As if she could, even if she wanted to.

Though, on second thought ...

She opened her map and quickly located the symbol for the restrooms. Nowhere close by, of course. Her finger traced the route that appeared to be the straightest shot, and then she jumped up and started that way. No time to let Nathan know where she'd gone. She'd deal with that later.

Pushing through the doorway, she sent up a thank you that the first stall was open.

Ten minutes later, her phone dinged.

Where are you?

She shifted into a different position, hoping the slight shift in equilibrium wouldn't send her right back. Her fingers trembled as she keyed in the few words. He was sure to be livid, but she couldn't help that now.

Bathroom just next to the entrance.

On my way.

When she was sure she wouldn't explode again for the moment, she splashed some water on her face and washed her mouth out as best as she could in the sink. As she slunk out of the restroom, her first sight was Nathan pacing nearby. He immediately grabbed her shoulders and examined her face. With gentle fingers, he brushed some hair from her cheek.

"You're sick."

She managed a small nod.

"C'mon." He handed her a water bottle and began to steer her out of the gates. "Back to the hotel."

Squeezing her eyes shut, she forced words out of her mouth she'd never wanted to have to admit to anyone. "I'm not sure I should risk getting in a car again yet." Especially not someone who didn't want to be married to her.

Nathan froze for a second, then nudged her forward again. "Well, we can't stay here, either. Not if you're sick."

"What—"

"Rest here for a moment while I turn the car on and let it cool off." He motioned toward the curb in front of the vehicle, shaded by a tree. "A hot car definitely won't help matters."

She opened the water and took a tiny sip.

"What else will you need?" He motioned toward the bottle she held. "Crackers? Ginger ale? Medicine?"

The thought of trying to eat anything else had her gagging again, but she forced her throat to behave. "Not right now."

"What can I do?"

"Get me back to the hotel?" She shrugged. "I think I'm just going to have to ride it out."

"There's got to be something—"

"Nathan." She waited until he looked her way. "The best thing for me right now is to be in a cool place close to a bathroom."

He nodded and opened her car door for her. "Let's get you back to the hotel, then."

Somehow, she made it through him swerving in the afternoon traffic and parking. He hovered over her a bit like a helicopter as they rode up in the elevator and walked down the hall to their rooms. Inside she slipped out of her shoes and pulled her hair back in a ponytail, so it would be easier if things started up again.

"What can I do to help?" Nathan still hovered just inside her door.

Bree shook her head. "I think whatever this is will just have to work its way out. Not much else to be done."

Her stomach gurgled once more, indicating a second maelstrom was about to strike. She jumped to her feet, pushed him out, and locked the door behind him. No way did she want her ex-fiancé to see her like this.

"Bree, let me in!" He banged on the door, but she couldn't have opened it at that moment even if she'd wanted to.

"Bree." Nathan's voice sounded close to tears when things eased up again several minutes later.

"I'll be okay, Nathan." Bree's voice was hoarse, but she projected it enough he could hear her. "I just need some time."

"I want to help."

"There's nothing you can do right now." She clutched at her middle where cramps and agony waged war.

Quiet was her only reply. Was he still out there? Had security come and hauled him away for making such a ruckus?

She rested her forehead against the tub's edge as tears ran down her cheeks. This elevator of a day could dock any time now. The joy of a new road trip had died almost as soon as it began.

And the only person here to take care of her was the one who didn't love her anymore.

9

That bird had a funny call. It sort of sounded like it was saying her name. Did woodpeckers sound like that? It sure was knocking on something a lot.

Bree peeled her eyes open one lid at a time. Where was she? The bathroom? Why was she sleeping in the floor with her head on the tub?

"Bree!" Nathan's voice came from the other side of the door. Not a bird.

"Hang on." Her voice came out scratchy, and she cringed at the coating on her tongue.

Shakily, she pushed to her knees and then the rest of the way up, using the sink for support. The mirror was harsher than usual, showing a line along her cheek from the edge of the bathtub. Her ponytail had fallen halfway down, and bits and pieces of the hair went every which way. She pushed it back up as neatly as she could and splashed some water on her face before daring to open the door.

No one stood in the hallway.

Had she imagined things? No. The tapping started again.

Bree spun around and searched. Was he knocking on the wall? Her gaze landed on the door between their rooms. Surely not.

Padding across the spongy carpet, she lifted a hand and touched the sliding lock. Should she? This door separating them this week echoed the rift that had grown between them since he called things off. If she removed this barrier, would it lead to other walls crumbling too? Did she want it to?

Nathan knocked again. "Bree? Bree, can you hear me?"

Taking a deep breath, she slid the metal bar back. With a twist of the knob, the door opened. Nathan practically fell through. Had he been leaning against it? He clasped her upper arm and pressed a hand to her forehead.

"Are you okay?"

"I've been better." The words croaked from her throat. "But maybe the worst has passed?"

He pulled her to his chest and cradled her there for a minute. "I was so scared. Why wouldn't you let me in?"

"I didn't want you to see me like that." She burrowed her face deeper into his shirt, muffling the words and her embarrassment at the same time. "Besides, it's not like I'm your responsibility or anything. Not anymore."

His muscles tightened. She could feel the hardness of them through his T-shirt. But he didn't let go where he held her, either.

What did that mean?

"Come here." He tugged her into his room and pressed her into a chair before motioning to grocery bags on the table. "Ginger ale, lemon-lime soda, peppermint tea, crackers, and any kind of stomach medicine I thought might be helpful."

"What in the world?" She peeked past the edge of a bag and pulled out a green bottle. "You did all this for me?"

"You wouldn't let me do anything else. I was willing to

hold your hair back or press a cool cloth to your face or whatever you might've needed, but you locked me out." He sank into the chair beside her. "I had to do something."

"Why?"

The question escaped before she thought it through, but now that it was out there, she wanted to know. Over the last few days, she'd seen so many different sides of this man. Which one was real?

"Why what?" Nathan stared over at the air conditioner as if it would provide answers.

"Why did you feel you had to do something? I mean, if anything, being sick was my own fault. I'm the one who insisted on the restaurant. Who dragged us around in the heat. Who ate more of that broccoli even after it didn't taste quite right."

Bree pressed a hand to her mouth and wrinkled her nose as her stomach protested the very thought of food. "And I don't think I'll be bringing that up again anytime soon. Ugh."

One corner of Nathan's lips twitched as if he fought a smile. "I won't bring it up either."

She waited, but he never returned to her earlier question. Did he still care for her? Should she press it?

"This might help settle some things a bit more." He leaned forward and twisted the top off her soda. "Some carbonation always makes me feel better when things are like that."

She took a tentative sip. "Thanks."

"You're welcome." He glanced around the room again. "I'm guessing you won't be wanting dinner tonight."

She swallowed hard before shaking her head. "But I don't want you to starve either."

"I'll be okay. If all else fails, I can nibble some of these crackers. I didn't get ahold of whatever it was you did, but that doesn't mean all this craziness hasn't affected me too."

"You're never going to eat Chinese again, are you?" Bree leaned back and crossed her arms.

"Not anytime soon." He lifted a brow. "Are you?"

"One bad experience shouldn't ruin a person's love for something." Or someone. Bree barely kept herself from following that train of thought.

She met his eyes, trying to discern if he was thinking anything similar. He blinked behind his dark glasses frames and pressed his lips together. He gave nothing else away.

"Anything else I can get you?" Nathan motioned toward the mess spread out between them.

"No. I think I'll probably just curl up in my bed and watch a sappy movie or something." She pushed out of her chair and tested her legs to see if they'd hold up enough to carry her back to the other side of the wall. "Earlier really sapped my energy."

"I can leave my side unlatched if you think you might need something in the night. Or I have my phone. Feel free to text." Nathan leaned in the opening between their two rooms.

"You're welcome to join me for the movie." What was she doing? "If you need to confirm that I really am feeling better. Or you just want the company."

"Oh, um." He ran a hand over the back of his neck. "I mean, I don't want to make you uncomfortable."

Bree squeezed her eyes closed against tears that threatened to escape. How many movies had they watched together over the last few years and never once been uneasy or awkward? She longed to find their way back to that. But was there even a road to get there, or had all the bridges been burned?

Maybe she could build one tonight.

"Come on, Nathan. It's just a movie. If anything, you'll probably be the one uncomfortable because I plan to watch a chick flick. And we both know how much you love those."

He grimaced, but she could tell it wasn't authentic. "In that case, maybe I'll just stay in my own room."

"Suit yourself." She fluffed a couple of pillows and set them against the headboard.

Nathan showed up at her elbow, another bottle of soda and some crackers in his arms. "Of course, I could just grab the remote control first."

Bree squeaked her protest. "Who's the sick one here?"

"I thought you said you were feeling better."

"I'm recovering." She snatched the device away from him and settled herself into the cocoon she'd made. "And it's my room."

As she scrolled through the options offered on the limited number of channels, she pondered the man beside her, his crumbs littering the bed. He was harder to predict than the Texas weather had been this week, and that was saying something. Because, before her last girls' trip, she would've sworn Nathan Hart was the steadiest man on earth.

Almost to a fault.

What had caused him to shift so dramatically?

Sometime during the movie, Bree had quit worrying about the distance between them. Or forgotten that there was any. Because now her head nestled on a pillow in Nathan's lap, her dark hair spilling over and tempting his fingers. What had he been thinking, following her in here and joining her on the bed, of all places?

Easing his legs into a more comfortable position, Nathan tried not to jostle her too much. He didn't want to steal the sleep she'd gained just as the hero kissed the girl for the first time. Probably better that way anyway. Romances didn't seem to work out in real life. Not in his experience, anyway.

His phone buzzed beside him.

Having a good time?

Josh. The good-for-nothing brother. What had he been thinking, setting them up to spend a week together on a cruise ship? And wouldn't he be surprised to find out how the week had really gone?

And how Nathan didn't plan to give in to any of their schemes or plans.

It's been interesting. Nothing like a hurricane to throw everything into chaos.

Now, to wait and see what Josh did with that reply. It didn't take long.

What? Are you okay?

Nathan startled to chuckle and then stifled it when Bree stirred.

Fine. Just spending a few days in Dallas instead of on a boat.

Though the thought of a boat had Nathan recalling some of the other ideas that had been thrown their way Sunday night. Had that only been twenty-four hours ago? What was it the man had said? Canoes? No. Something foreign.

Gondolas.

He quickly typed in a search and found the website. Whew! They were proud of their boat rides, evidently. More than he'd typically pay to do something like that. Not that he'd ever done anything like that, but still. If he were to ...

Hm.

Maybe a broader search would show him some other ideas of things to do. Including some that didn't cost so much money. The way they'd been spending it the last few days was sending him into the beginnings of cardiac arrest.

Cattle.

No.

More museums.

After the disaster that morning, that didn't hold any appeal.

Lakes.

Shopping.

Aquarium.

Roller coasters.

Blah. Most of that could be done in Tennessee. There had to be something different to do around here.

Bree was so much better at this than he was, but she was sick. And the idea of surprising her sent warm fuzzies through him. A feeling he wasn't about to evaluate any closer.

Why did you stay in Dallas if your cruise got canceled?

Josh's text interrupted Nathan's browsing.

Playing the tourist before I head back east. Never been to Dallas before.

Now his brother was sure to suspect something. Nathan never willingly played the tourist. That was always Bree's thing. Maybe that's why he'd been so eager to jump on the cruise idea. Everything was already planned, so all he had to do was buy the tickets and show up.

Bree's original idea of spending a week in New York City had lots of merit, but it was also overwhelming. A million different things to do there, from the Statue of Liberty to Central Park to shopping to the Empire State Building. How was he supposed to know which was the best part of the city to stay in or what to allow time for?

And yet, now he was trying to do something similar in a city even less familiar to him. His thumb hovered to scroll again but froze. There was an idea with merit. Even something she might have done in New York, had they gone there. And not ridiculously expensive.

Alone?

Josh's text came through right before the phone started ringing. Nathan eased out from under Bree as quickly as he could without waking her, no easy feat as his legs had fallen asleep. He pressed the button to answer right before the call would've gone to voice mail.

"Not even going to give a guy time to type in an answer?" Nathan pushed the door on his side most of the way closed so his lowered voice wouldn't carry as much.

"Nope. I needed to hear you say it."

"Say what?"

"Nathan, you're not the kind of guy who decides to play tourist on a whim." Josh's voice was full of sarcasm and something else.

"Oh, really?" Nathan leaned against the window and stared out at the parking lot. "And what kind of guy am I?"

"The kind who jumps on a plane for home as soon as he can and then sits and licks his wounds."

Nathan flinched at the image. Not that he'd ever admit it was accurate. His brother needed no encouragement to continue.

"Is Bree with you?"

Nathan bit back what he wanted to say. "Why would Bree be with me? We broke up, remember?"

Josh huffed. "I remember you messing up that perfect bit of paradise you found yourself in by calling off the wedding. I don't remember her having much say in it."

"Remember it however you want to, Little Brother. That doesn't change facts."

Would Josh let the subject change? As Bree had earlier when she questioned his desire to take care of her—though Nathan could tell she hadn't wanted to. Not that he'd been able to formulate an answer anyway. He wasn't sure of the reason himself.

Why had he wanted so desperately to make sure she was okay?

When he returned to the empty bench where he'd left her, panic had filled every single inch of his six-foot frame. Her reply had answered the where, but he hadn't expected the paleness or dark circles under her eyes when she came out of the bathroom. It was as though live wires had given him a jump start and he'd had to move, to do anything and everything he could to revive at least a little of the *joi de vivre* she usually wore like an outfit.

"Earth to Nathan. Are you still there?" Josh's voice jerked him back to the present.

"I'm here." He dropped the curtain and perched on the edge of his bed.

"You going to answer my question?"

"You going to admit you're a scheming, lying, conniving brat of a brother?" Nathan shot back, tired of the game.

"So, you've at least seen her."

"Yes. Quite the shock that was too. Getting ready to sit and wait for the plane only to run into the one person I thought I'd never see again." Nathan tugged on a strand of hair that was almost too long and hung over his forehead. "Thanks for the warning."

"If I'd warned you, you'd never have gone on the cruise."

"I never got to go on the cruise anyway."

"Moot point." Josh's voice firmed up, as if he were a parent instead of a brother. "I wasn't trying to shock you. I just wanted you to spend some time together again and remember why you loved Bree in the first place. Because I can't figure out why you would push aside the best thing that ever happened to you. And I wanted you to reconsider before you made the worst mistake of your life."

"Sometimes you don't know as much as you think you do."

"So, tell me."

Nathan wavered for a moment. Should he? How could Josh not know at least as much as Nathan did? They'd grown up in the same house, seen the same things, experienced the same history. But Josh was younger. Maybe he didn't remember as clearly.

"Let it go, Josh. I'll be home in a few days, and maybe we can talk then."

"Nathan—"

Nathan ended the call before his brother could say anything else. He was worse than an old woman, trying to fix a presumed wrong. But in this case, Nathan had made the right decision, and he planned to stick with it.

As he got ready to plug in his phone for the night, he noticed the website still open for the activity he'd been considering. He glanced back toward Bree's room. She'd enjoy it. He knew that much. But was it a good idea in the long run?

10

Ringing.

What was ringing?

Nathan struggled to pry his eyes open, but they complained about the process for a minute. Where was he again? He squinted around the space, blinking a few times to try and clear things up—at least as much as they would without his glasses.

"Hello?" A sleepy voice nearby had him blinking even harder and fumbling around for those glasses. Was someone in his room?

"Katie? Do you know what time it is?" Bree. It was Bree's voice.

Everything clicked into place. He'd left the door between their rooms cracked the night before just in case she needed anything. His gaze narrowed in on the clock, and he flopped back on the pillow again. It wasn't that early for a normal day, but he'd had trouble getting to sleep the night before.

"Caribbean? No. That's not what I meant." Footsteps padded across the carpet in the next room.

Nathan resisted trying to peek through the small slit for a glimpse of her.

"Oh. No. I'm not on the cruise." The sound of something smacking skin came through—probably Bree bopping herself in the forehead, like she tended to do when remembering something she'd meant to do before. "No. There was a hurricane."

The conversation sounded familiar. Much like what he'd gone through with Josh the night before.

"Dallas. Nothing was flying out anyway, and the cruise was a bust, so I just decided to explore a new city." Bree's voice had quickly regained its normal perkiness.

He'd never been able to understand how she could be so ... *awake* without any coffee or anything. Ironic, since she always said he was a morning person. Maybe she'd just never seen him before coffee. Bree's laugh interrupted his getting up to start some caffeine. Had Katie been in on the match-making scheme, too, or just Skye and Josh?

"Why do you say that?" Bree's voice held a note of wariness.

Nathan really should go push the door closed and quit listening, but he couldn't seem to take a step.

"Yeah ... I saw Nathan." There was something in the way Bree said it that he couldn't interpret.

If only he could see her.

"Mm, hmm. We bumped into each other at the airport. What on earth were you thinking trying to send us off for a week on a boat together? And did you ever stop to think that we'd have had to share a room?"

Nathan's heart escalated. There had been many times over the last year that sharing a room with Bree had been a dream, but he'd given that up when he called things off. Even though he'd still had moments over the last few days where the attraction was strong, it wasn't stronger than his willpower.

Thank God for the hurricane that kept them from being trapped in more temptation than they already had.

"No, Katie. I don't think ship captains will perform marriage ceremonies on a whim anymore. Pretty sure you still need a license to get married even at sea. And besides, he doesn't seem to want to head back in the direction of marriage."

She finally walked into his line of sight, her hand twisting her ponytail around and around as she paced. Even first thing in the morning, she was gorgeous.

"Yes, he's with me, though I don't know why." Bree froze. "What? No! *Separate* hotel rooms."

Nathan stood to go close the door. He'd let himself eavesdrop too long as it was.

"No. It was his idea to stay, actually. Something about me proving what a road trip was like with boys tagging along. I don't know how I'm supposed to prove anything when it's nothing like the road trip with you guys."

Fingers on the handle, he froze. For some reason, he needed to hear more.

"I don't know, Katie. He's got me completely confused. I still can't understand what made him call everything off. He said he doesn't trust me, but he acts more like he doesn't trust himself."

Nathan's heart fell to his bare feet. Her words rang truer than just about anything he'd heard or thought in a while. But how could that be?

On the other side of the room, his daily alarm began to jangle, jerking him from his stupor and sending him flying across the bed.

Bree gasped. "I didn't realize the door was open still. No, Katie. It was nothing like that. I got—"

And then the door closed and muffled her voice too much to make anything out. Nathan pressed a palm to his forehead. Did she realize how much he'd heard? How awkward would things be for the rest of the day? Not to mention the drive home tomorrow.

Nothing he could do about it now. He pushed back to a sitting position and looked around the still-dark room. Time to face the day, ready or not.

Coffee. And a shower. Those should make everything else look better, right? He could hope anyway.

When Bree still hadn't texted or anything half an hour later, he decided just to act like he hadn't overheard her conversation earlier and make first contact.

Hungry? I'm thinking about heading down to see what's on the breakfast bar.

The words were easy enough to type, though a bit harder to send. It was just breakfast. More than likely cereal or bagels. Nothing fancy. He pushed the button, and a moment later, the phone told him his message had been received.

Give me five more minutes and I'll join you.

Okay.

He let out a breath he hadn't realized he'd been holding.

They stepped out of their rooms at almost the same moment. A laugh holding a bit of nervousness slipped from him. She fell into step beside him, and they remained quiet on the elevator. And all the way through preparing their plates of food and finding a table.

"Sleep okay?" He broke the silence before biting into a muffin.

"Must have. I didn't wake up until my phone went off this morning." Bree watched him, but he tried to school his features to give nothing away.

"That's good. Maybe the worst of what hit you yesterday afternoon is over, then."

"Hopefully." Bree spooned some yogurt into her mouth and narrowed her eyes. "Have you heard from anyone back home?"

"Home? Like Tennessee where I live or Texarkana where I came from?" He studied his banana as if it held all the answers in the world.

"Either, I guess."

"Josh called last night. Wanted to know if I was having fun on the cruise."

"How funny." Bree opened her granola bar. "Katie called me this morning asking the same thing."

"Think they're in cahoots?"

"Evidently have been for weeks now. Katie and Skye got the information and tickets from Josh in the first place." She sipped her juice. "I'm not sure what they were thinking."

"Obviously they weren't." Nathan pushed his plate away.

"Right." Bree crumbled up the last few bites onto her plate. "I mean, I guess they meant well ... but ..."

"Yeah." He pointed to her leftovers. "You done?"

She nodded.

"Up for a bit of an adventure?" He dropped their trash in the can and then waited for her to stand.

"Adventure?" Bree raised an eyebrow. "Like what?"

"I was looking some stuff up last night, trying to figure out what to do today. I might have an idea of something you'd enjoy."

Her blue eyes searched his face, a wrinkle between the brows.

"What?" He ran a hand over his chin, but all he felt was a bit of stubble he'd missed when shaving. He always had trouble catching the part right above his Adam's apple.

"I don't know." Bree started walking again. "So, where are we going?"

"You'll see."

No going back now. He'd brought it up and now had to fulfill the promise of something fun. And he knew she'd like it. It was just a matter of not giving in to his friends' and brother's hopes and wishes. Because that's all they could be.

———

"Where are we going again?" Bree craned her neck as they meandered past old warehouses and other brick structures.

"You'll see."

"But you think this is something I'll enjoy?" She cut her eyes sideways at him. What on earth could be in this area that she'd enjoy?

The corner of his lips turned up in a smirk as he parked. "Pretty certain. Ready?"

"As I'll ever be, considering I still don't know what to expect."

He held her door and then pointed them in the right direction. "Come on. Should just be a few blocks this way."

"Where are we, exactly? Somewhere close to the Kennedy museum, right?"

"Right." He glanced at her as if impressed. "This is the West End. It evidently used to be a bunch of warehouses and railway buildings, but it had a facelift and now has a bunch of shops and restaurants and bars. But that's not why we're here this morning."

"You didn't want to go shopping?" She couldn't resist teasing him a little.

"Not really." He pointed down the street. "How about doing something like that instead?"

A carriage sat on the side of the road, the horse waiting patiently. It wasn't Central Park, but it was something she'd mentioned wanting to do. She blinked and then turned wide eyes his way.

"A carriage ride?" Her voice came out much higher than normal, the excitement leaking through.

"Yes."

"What are we waiting for?" She pulled him forward, practically bouncing with each step.

The driver nodded, accepted their payment, and helped her into the white equipage. Bree settled in and looked back his way, but Nathan remained on the sidewalk. A visible war raged across his face, as if he couldn't quite talk himself into climbing in with her.

"Oh no." She pointed at him. "You're not getting out of this. It was your idea, and you're coming with me."

He hesitated one more second and then shook his head. "I don't have to. This was something you wanted to do. Probably be more fun without me."

"Get your hind end up here in this comfy seat, or I'm climbing back down."

The driver probably considered them the craziest couple he'd ever seen, but she couldn't help that. Regardless of anyone or anything else around them, Nathan was being ridiculous, and she wasn't about to let him get away with it. She started to stand, but he jumped in before she could. She slid back down as he settled himself as far away as possible on the bench.

A lump of disappointment settled in her chest. Just over a month ago, she'd watched Katie climb into a carriage much like this one, Camden accompanying her. They'd known each other only half a day at that point, but he'd sat closer and been sweeter than the man next to Bree now. The one she'd known and loved for years.

Their coach rolled along at a lazy pace, allowing them to admire all the old brick structures around them.

"This is lovely, Nathan." Maybe talking about normal things would ease some of the tension.

"Agreed."

Or not. "What gave you the idea?"

"I was scrolling through websites that listed things to do in Dallas, and this one caught my eye. Made me think of New York City for some reason."

Bree couldn't help the grin that took over. Even when he didn't want to, he still remembered things she'd mentioned wanting to do in New York. Could there be a few warm feelings toward her left inside him? She kept getting a glimpse of something in his eyes, only to have it hidden again.

This morning, had he heard any of her phone conversation with Katie? Did he know the turmoil she was going through, trying to figure out what he wanted from these days together? Because if he did want the relationship ended for good, wouldn't it be easier just to sever the cords and never see each other again? This ... forcing time together when nothing could come of it—it was agony.

"Look at those shops. Don't they look interesting?" Bree purposely leaned Nathan's way, testing to see what he'd do.

He didn't shift, but he didn't look like he wanted her to linger either. "Mm. Shops."

Right. So much for that. She slid back to her side.

In front of them, a giant tower loomed over the city, its top a giant, sparkly globe.

"What is that?" Nathan tilted his head.

"Reunion Tower." She nudged his side with her elbow. "A restaurant that revolves so you can see the whole city. Didn't they mention it when they tossed out ideas Sunday night?"

"For some reason, that's not what I imagined it looking like."

"Whyever not?" With her pointer finger, she circled the air. "It makes sense, structurally. And I think you can go up even if you don't eat at the restaurant."

"It's ... high."

"Yep."

And he was afraid of heights. She'd discovered that during a weekend trip in college when they'd gone hiking with some other friends. He'd about had a heart attack when she stepped closer to a ledge than he considered safe. Would he still be so worried about her now?

The carriage turned and took them back towards where they began, passing Dealy Plaza and its memorial, a big red brick building that was some other sort of museum—although it looked almost castle-like—and more revitalized warehouses.

"There's a spaghetti restaurant that's supposed to be amazing. We could try it later today if you want." Nathan motioned toward her side of the carriage.

"We'll see. Not sure if my stomach can handle tomato sauce yet."

He nodded.

And then they were back where they started. The breeze, stirred up while they toured through the streets, calmed, and the eighty degrees wrapped around them, promising even more warmth as the day went on. About as delightful as spending the rest of the daylight hours with the curmudgeon who'd ridden beside her.

Nathan held out his hand to help her down. She paused a moment, then accepted his assistance. And his fingers still felt strong and safe and perfect around hers. More bittersweet than her granny's favorite brownie recipe.

"Where to next?" She glanced around, hoping something would catch her eye.

"I don't know, honestly. Nothing else really sounded good to me when I weighed various options last night. I hoped you'd have some ideas."

"What are y'all lookin' for?" The driver interrupted their conversation. "Anything in particular?"

Bree threw an appreciative smile his way. "We're just exploring the city a bit. This is our first time in Dallas, and we're playing tourist."

"But we've already done some things." Nathan interrupted. "And we're hoping for some more budget-friendly options too."

"Well, I was going to suggest the aquarium on a hot day like this, but that's not budget-friendly unless you have a season pass. Nor the zoo." He lifted his cap and scratched his thinning hair. "There's a park somewhere around here. Clyde-Warren or something like that. Has some fun things. And it's free, far as I know. Of course, there's all them murals over in Deep Ellum. Was a big article about it in the Sunday paper. Or we have several lakes and such."

"Thanks so much." Bree passed him a few dollars for a tip. "And for the ride too. Your carriage and horse are lovely."

"Nothing to it." He tipped his hat and nodded before turning to wait for other customers.

"So, did any of that sound good?" Bree followed Nathan back down the sidewalk toward the car.

"I mean, I don't know." Nathan looked more at the concrete under his feet than anything around them.

"Here." Bree paused in a shady spot and pulled out her phone. A quick search found the park the man had mentioned.

"Okay. Klyde Warren Park. Not exactly Central Park—it's only 5.2 acres instead of 843, but it is a place with things to do. Looks like it has some food trucks, too, so we could eat lunch there."

"You know how many acres are in Central Park just off the top of your head?"

She lifted a brow. "I was researching New York with the thoughts of going on a honeymoon. I soaked up a bit of information over the last year."

"I guess I'm game to check out this other park if you are." Nathan glanced away and twirled the car keys around his finger. "Shall we?"

"Why not?" Bree rolled her eyes. "After all, it's free—your favorite price range—except for probably a parking meter fee."

"Just because I'm thrifty doesn't make me a bad person."

"Never said it did." Bree slid into the hot car. "But sometimes you need to remember there are more important things in life than money."

Nathan cringed as if she'd slapped him. What had she said but the truth? It took him longer than usual to walk around the back of the vehicle before sliding into the driver's seat. He gripped the wheel, his jaw set.

"Got the navigation pulled up?" His voice was steel, cold and firm.

How on earth had she made him this mad with one little reprimand? And what did that mean for the rest of their day?

11

He didn't say another word the whole way to the park. Bree fidgeted on her side of the car. If only she could find the guy she'd fallen in love with three years before. He had to be locked away inside this stranger sitting next to her.

Pulling in beside a meter, Nathan dug in his pocket for some change.

"I can cover it." Bree pulled out her wallet.

He shot her a glare that had her quickly shoving it back into her bag.

Note to self—don't talk about money with Nathan. Ever. Again.

"Should be this way." He pointed down the street. "Shall we?"

Nodding, she followed his lead. Several blocks later, a green space stretched out before them ... and over a freeway. Her mouth hung open like a fish, but she didn't care.

As if he were a game show host, Nathan gestured across the street. "Klyde Warren Park, at your service."

"Wow." She had no other words. She pointed to the *walk*

sign and tugged him into the intersection. Now that she could see it, she was ready to explore.

"Where should we start?"

They halted at the entrance, looking left and right. A plaza stood in front of them, water splashing somewhere nearby. The sounds of laughter, conversation, and traffic were all around, but the park itself was like an oasis in the middle of the busy city.

"What all is there to do?" She glanced around and saw a kiosk with maps. "Here."

He looked over her shoulder as she held up the paper with a bit of information about what they could find.

"Food trucks, butterfly garden, kids' area, pavilions and walkways, games for rent?" Her voice went up in pitch with each item listed. If she lived in Dallas, she'd want to come here every day.

"Well, since breakfast wasn't that long ago, we probably don't need to start with the food trucks."

"Ugh. You're right." Although the coffee one in her line of sight smelled amazing.

"Should we start heading toward one end and just work our way around?"

"Sounds like as good a plan as any."

"Let's do it, then." He veered to the left and walked down a pathway under white arches spaced every few feet.

As they strolled, some of the tension from before slipped from his shoulders. She wasn't sure what had caused it in the first place or where it had gone, but she sure didn't want a repeat. She'd just thank God for the relief and try to enjoy the rest of this outing.

Near the back of the park, Bree read a sign for the next section. "Oh, a Botanical Garden."

"Didn't I just take you to the Arboretum to see flowers yesterday?"

Had that only been the day before? Seemed like a lifetime ago. "A girl can never see too many flowers."

"I'll try to remember that."

There. That was more like the man she used to know. The one she'd meant to spend the rest of forever with.

Fighting past the glimmer of hope, Bree pretended she hadn't noticed and pointed. "Besides, these are all supposedly native ones. We might learn something."

He rolled his eyes but followed her into the little landscaped area full of Texas plants. She didn't point out that she recognized several from the Arboretum. That would probably just bring up that he'd wasted his money on a place like that when they could have come here instead, or some malarky of the kind.

Near the back of the garden, juvenile laughter had Bree wanting to join in. "We must be near the children's play area."

"Sounds that way."

"There was a children's part at the Arboretum, too, but it was at the other end from where we explored." She rounded the corner and caught a glimpse of the ones making the happy sounds.

"Doesn't really make sense for us to wander through a children's section, though." Nathan stuck his hands in his pockets. "Not like we have any."

Nor would they. No. Dreams of little boys with rumpled hair the same brown as his had died along with all the rest of that fairy tale. No silvery blue eyes. No mathematicians. No future at all for the two of them.

So, why couldn't she accept that?

"That is a cool tree house, though." Bree watched the

happy families dashing around the play area for another minute. "Shall we continue?"

"Sure."

In the big yard to their right, more families played soccer, threw frisbees, and even attempted to fly a kite. Up ahead, a kiosk boasted a variety of games and other stands offered books and magazines for reading. Tables were clustered on a paved area, and music played somewhere nearby.

"Games, Nathan!"

"Games." One word, but it didn't sound promising. More like she'd suggested they wrestle snakes.

"You don't like games?" She turned to him, hands on her hips.

"Not really."

"Seriously? How did I not know this about you?"

He shrugged. "I guess we've never really had a chance to talk about it. I mean, I know you played games with the girls in your dorm, but it was always after lobby hours were over, so I never had to join in."

"Huh."

"I assume you're going to want to rent one of these games?" He pointed to a couple tables nearby. "Or challenge me to a round of Chess or Connect 4? That has to be the biggest Connect 4 set I've ever seen."

The game was as big as one of those old chalkboards with wheels. The disks to go in the slots were as big as her hand. A little thrill went up her spine at the potential, but he obviously wasn't feeling the same way.

"I don't want to make you miserable." Her voice took on a pouty tone all on its own—one that could either win him over or drive him crazy.

"I can stand playing a game for a little while even if it's not my favorite thing in the world." He started toward the kiosk, then turned back, raising a finger. "But keep in mind I have a mathematical brain and that tends to help in games of strategy."

"Right." Bree giggled. "And I have a childlike mind, which helps even more."

"You've got to be kidding me."

"I am. Mostly." She rushed past him to the kiosk to check out the options. Several word games, some cards, a few of the truth-or-dare types she knew he'd hate.

"Whatcha lookin' for today, hon?" The lady working the stand smiled at her. "We've got a little bit of everything and not many checked out so far."

"Sort of just seeing what's available. This is our last day in Dallas, and we're soaking up as much as we can. Someone suggested we come spend some time in this park, and it's beautiful."

"Have you seen the other side? There's ping pong over there. And shuffleboard." The lady pointed to the east side.

"No. We've only been around this way so far. I might just challenge him to the giant Connect 4 over there, and then we can go try our hands at ping pong."

"Sounds like a plan. You enjoy our beautiful city."

"Thanks so much." Bree pushed away and searched for Nathan, but he must have overheard her conversation because he was staking out one of the large game pieces.

"Red or black?"

"Red, of course." She grabbed her bag of disks. "Does that mean you go first, or me?"

"Youngest first?" He raised an eyebrow.

"Fine with me." She dropped her first circle right in the middle.

"Not playing from the edges, huh?" He claimed the far right.

"Nope. I have a strategy." She went straight on top of her last one.

"Is it what I think it is?" He followed her example with his own piece.

"You'll have to wait and see." She moved to the next slot over and dropped her third piece in.

"Hmm." He hesitated and then went ahead and stacked his color three up.

She had to block him then, of course. Couldn't let him win so easily. Not until she'd beaten him a few times, at least.

"Okay." He tapped his piece against his chin while he considered where to go next. Once more, he mimicked her and went right next to his first column.

Back to her original plan, she placed one on the other side of her original column. Several rounds later, she had a triangle where all she had to do was place one more and she'd get four one way or another. And he couldn't stop her.

"Really?" He hovered his disk above the various slots but was having trouble making up his mind.

"Sometimes it pays to play lots of games because you learn to strategize better." She giggled as she slid in her winning piece.

"Oh, is that the reason to play games? I thought it was to have fun." He reached over and tweaked her nose.

"Did you have fun?"

One end of his lips tilted up. It was enough. He might deny it out loud, but deep inside, he enjoyed himself.

"So, ping pong, huh?"

"Might as well." She glanced at his watch. "It's too early for lunch yet."

Nathan didn't tell Bree he'd had plenty of practice at ping pong in his own dorm over the last few years. She might have bested him at Connect 4, but that didn't mean he didn't have a few tricks up his sleeve. He wasn't the most athletic person in the world, but he could get around a ping pong table quickly enough.

On the first serve, the ball flew past her, leaving her spinning. "Whoa!"

"Not too bad, huh?"

She chased the little white orb and brought it back, a sudden timidness to her movements. "Okay, then. Here we go."

Her serve was sloppy, but the ball made it to his side, and he lobbed it back. She managed to return it but missed when he sent it back her way even faster.

"Two for you."

"Sounds good to me." He gave the ball a bounce and served it once more.

After he was up ten and she had yet to get it by him, she announced him the winner.

"Do you quit so easily?" He laid the paddle down on the table for the next person to enjoy.

"Only when I know there's no way I'll win." She came over and tilted her head as she studied him. "Where did you learn to play like that? And don't tell me you're just a natural."

"I'm not a natural. But I had some suitemates who were pretty vicious in the basement after curfew. When we needed a study break, we headed down there and played while our laundry dried." He pointed to the other end of the park. "Do you want to walk the rest of the way around before we head over to the food trucks?"

"I guess."

"Looks like another garden of some sort."

"A butterfly garden!" She meandered into the flowers, her bright shirt blending in with some areas.

"I don't see any butterflies."

"The point of a butterfly garden is to grow plants the butterflies like. Then, they come of their own free will. It's not actually where they grow butterflies." She pointed. "But there's one."

Sure enough, looking closer, he saw several fluttering around. "Interesting."

"I'd love to do a butterfly garden. You haven't seen Katie's sister's yard, but she has one, and it's gorgeous. I could ask her advice." Bree buried her nose in a bush with purple blooms.

He could picture her having a backyard like this. Full of color and life. With kids running around. And laughter.

Why did such a happy image elicit such sadness?

Because he wouldn't be there. And it was his own fault. He shook the thought from his head. No regrets. This was for the good of both of them.

They meandered through the flowers a few more minutes, Bree snapping a few pictures as she discovered a different butterfly or flower than she'd seen before. Enough clouds floated across the sky that the heat wasn't as oppressive as the day before. And a breeze brought a bit of relief too. Nathan could stand a few more minutes in the sun if that kept up.

She finally straightened and pointed to the restrooms nearby. "I need to stop here before we eat."

"Sounds good. I should probably go put a few more coins in the meter anyway. Meet you over at those tables?" He indicated the area near the food trucks.

"Sure."

It didn't take him long to walk the few blocks back to pay the meter a bit more and return. No sign of Bree yet, so he propped himself on the edge of a picnic table and pulled out his phone. A work email notification caught his eye.

Sure, he had it set to send out an out-of-office notification, but this one looked like an easy answer for a pretty important client he hadn't been able to reach the week before. It would take him only a few seconds to reply. His thumb hovered momentarily and then tapped to open the message.

"Are you working?" Bree's voice froze him in the middle of typing out his reply. "On vacation?"

"I was waiting on you, and this will only take a second."

"It couldn't wait two more days?"

He dared a glance up and could see the hurt written in her eyes. "What?"

"You realize you're not supposed to work on vacation, right?" She shook her head.

"Oh, for crying out loud!" He hissed, fighting his rising ire. "It seriously would only take a minute to send that email for one of our bigger clients. Otherwise I wouldn't have touched it."

"Is it urgent?"

"What?"

"Is the email something urgent? Or could it have waited?"

This was ridiculous. "Look, just because teachers get to take the summer off, it doesn't mean everyone else does. Sometimes accountants have to send emails or take a phone call even when they're on vacation. It's not that big of a deal."

"It is that big of a deal." Bree slashed her hand through the air. "Do you realize this is why Skye is the way she is?"

"What?" How had they gone from his sending an email to Bree's road trip buddy?

"Skye's dad works all the time. He never takes any time off. She won't admit it, but I think it's what's holding her back from finding a job of her own. She's so afraid she's going to become just like that."

Nathan shook his head. "Just because I'm sending one email doesn't mean I'll end up like that. I'm new to the firm, and this is one of my biggest clients. I figured it would be a courtesy to let him know I was going to look into his problem as soon as I get back."

"You didn't have an out-of-office message?" Bree frowned.

"I did, but, like I said, this is one of my first big clients. I'm just trying to make a good impression."

"Well, I hope you impressed your client. Because you haven't impressed me." Bree pinched her lips together for a moment. "And maybe it's a good thing we're not getting married after all. Because I wouldn't want to live with a man who could never take time off from work."

There it was. What he'd been trying to make her see for a month now.

Nathan couldn't speak. Shards of ache shattered his chest.

Something he'd been hoping to hear shouldn't hurt this much.

12

His fingers gripped the edge of the picnic table he'd perched on earlier.

Bree slapped a hand over her mouth, her blue eyes wide. Regret was written on her face as plainly as if tattooed there. But he couldn't let her repent what she'd just said. After all, he'd decided they weren't meant to be married over a month ago. Her finally agreeing was perfect.

Right?

"Good." He peeled his fingers away from the wood grain one at a time.

"Good?" Bree's voice came out as a squeak.

"Yes. Good. Good that we're not getting married since we're so obviously unsuitable for each other."

He hopped off the table and walked toward the food trucks, not waiting to see if she followed or not. Emotions rolled through him like the world's worst-designed roller coaster. His stomach churned, arguing against finding something to eat.

But he needed a distraction, and this was all that came to mind.

"Nathan, wait." Bree huffed up beside him, her shorter legs taking three steps for every one of his.

"It's lunchtime. I thought I'd go get some lunch." He refused to look at her.

"Nathan." She grabbed his arm and tugged, her feet digging into the soft grass. "Please."

A familiar pounding began in his temples.

Not now.

Pressing his knuckles to either side of his head, he closed his eyes for a moment, willing the tension to ease up. Not that the trick had ever worked on his migraines before, but there was a first time for everything. Though, apparently, not this go round. He needed caffeine, stat.

He squinted as he opened his eyes again, the Texas sunlight seeming brighter than ever. "Let's get some lunch."

Bree followed, not saying a word.

Studying the options, he weighed the pros and cons of each. Anything with meat sent his stomach into fits. Fish didn't sound much better. Definitely not tacos.

Hm. Mac 'n cheese might sit okay. The cheese would give a little protein, and the pasta shouldn't be too terribly heavy.

Of course, a food truck didn't carry just plain old regular macaroni. Oh no. There was some with truffle oil, some with four different specialty cheeses, bacon, and apples, of all things. He pursed his lips as he debated between the flavors available.

"What about that one?" Bree pointed near the top. He'd almost forgotten she was there.

Mama's Mac 'n Cheese. It was as plain as this place got anyway, despite the description including aged cheddar and homemade breadcrumbs. It would have to do.

He ordered a small helping of the pasta and the largest soda they had. Bree placed her order right after, but he didn't listen. Instead, he found a small square of shade to the side of the truck and waited there, hoping it would be a bit cooler.

"Do we need to go back to the hotel so you can cool off?" Bree pulled him from wishes for ice packs and mentholated cream.

He hadn't thought to pack anything like that. Hadn't expected to get blindsided by a migraine on vacation since his normally came from stress. Of course, this had to be the most stressful vacation ever.

"Nathan?" A guy waved out the open window of the food truck. "Order up."

Grabbing the warm dish and the cool drink, he immediately pressed the side of the cup to his forehead. It didn't do much, but it did help some. Bree's order came quickly after his.

"Hey. Hotel?" Bree touched his arm more gently than he knew possible.

"No. It's okay to stay here and eat." He'd already ruined the morning. No need to mess up her lunch too.

"You're sure?"

"Sure."

They settled at a picnic table in a shaded area. Bree took a bite and closed her eyes as she chewed. Whatever she'd ordered must've been good. And despite his pounding head, he couldn't tear his gaze away from her lips where a string of cheese hung on for dear life.

"What?"

He blinked and met her stare. "Sorry. Phased out there for a moment."

One of her eyebrows rose higher than the other, but she didn't push it.

He got a few bites down before replacing the lid on his dish. Maybe he could save the rest for later this afternoon. But the way things were getting hazy around the edges of his vision, he didn't want to push eating too much just now.

Should he have agreed when she suggested they head back before eating? The thought of driving through lunch-hour traffic in this state held absolutely no pleasure for him. But he'd pushed through doing all sorts of things with a migraine before. He could do it again.

"How long have you been hurting?" Bree's question didn't register at first.

Hurting? Did she mean from what she'd said earlier? How long his heart had ached and throbbed and only gotten worse since spending the last few days with the woman he wished he could allow himself to love?

"Is it a headache?"

Headache was a mild term for it. *Vice grip of wrath* sounded closer, although it still lacked some of the vengeance and agony being wrought on his cerebrum right now.

"Nathan, how long have you had a migraine?" Bree tilted her head to meet his stare.

Oh. Right. "Just a little while."

"You're pretty pale."

"It's getting worse quicker than I expected." Under normal circumstances, he wouldn't have admitted that, but the pain hindered his defenses.

"Come on." Bree dumped her trash and tugged on his arm until he stood. "Give me the keys."

"No." He shook his head. "I can drive."

"You can barely see straight." She pointed to his pocket. "Now, are you going to hand them over, or do I have to go in after them?"

Much as that thought would've been welcome in a different scenario, there was no way he was letting it happen now. He shoved his hand deep into his pocket but didn't pull it out right away. While he knew she was probably right about being the better one to drive right now, it still pinched his ego to have to let her.

"Nathan Everette Hart." Bree already had a mom voice down, which was completely unfair, all things considered.

He inched the keys out and dropped them in her open palm. She scooped up his leftovers and handed him his drink. Without a word, she slipped her arm through one of his and steered them toward the exit.

Beyond demeaning. And if an orchestra-sized drum set weren't going off behind his eyeballs, he might put up more of a fight. As it was, he was doing well to walk in a straight line, even with her guiding him.

"Your chariot awaits." Bree opened the passenger door and motioned inside.

Glaring at her, he slid into the sauna anyway, cringing when he barked his shin against the glove compartment.

"Hang in there." Bree scooted the driver's seat up to where she could reach the pedals. "GPS says about fifteen minutes. Just close your eyes. The air will cool off in a minute."

Her voice was calm and quiet. Soothing, just like it had been every time he'd had one of these during college—usually during midterms and finals. She'd sit in his lobby and run her fingers through his hair, helping some of the tension ebb away. It hadn't completely cured them or anything, but it did make them bearable. He'd missed her.

She hit the brakes harder than normal, and he grimaced. No way was he about to open his eyes. It was hard enough relinquishing control as it was—looking would only make it worse. His fingers wrapped around the edge of his seat cushion, and he breathed in and out as deeply as he could.

Without opening his eyes, he knew they were back simply because the parking garage was darker. His aching head was grateful. If only he didn't have to go through the bright lobby to get to his room. Bree opened his door and slid her arm through his once more before they walked to the elevators.

Why was she being so nice? And after everything said earlier. He didn't understand.

"You get some rest. I know that helps more than anything." Bree paused before his door. "Do you need anything before I go back to my room?"

Much as he wanted to ask her to come run her fingers through his hair and press a cold cloth to his forehead, he knew he shouldn't. He'd knocked that bridge down. Instead, he managed to shake his head enough that she could see the negative reply.

With that, she was gone, the door clicking shut behind her. He barely held in the groan of frustration and anguish that longed to escape. Of all the things to inherit from his father— and there was a long list he hadn't wanted—this was the worst.

Nothing to do now but ride it out. Three of the strongest painkillers on hand would have to do since he hadn't packed his other meds. He lay down, holding himself stiff, not wanting to move more than absolutely necessary, trying to keep his breaths regular and even. And with each inhale, he sent up a prayer that the drugs would kick in on the next exhale.

———

Bree hugged her knees to her chest, her back against the headboard of her bed. Nathan had some doozies of migraines while they dated, but she'd never seen one hit this fast. It had to be her fault.

Why had she said that awful thing? She hadn't even really meant it. But it slipped out before she could stop it.

"I'm so stupid."

Her head crashed into her knees, sending a bit of pain through her own skull.

Nothing compared to the ache that had resided in her chest for a month now. The continual radiating spirals of hurt and loneliness. And today, it had come out in anger.

Anger at herself for still loving him even when he didn't want her to.

Anger at him for deciding to stay and follow her around this week.

Anger at Skye and Josh and Katie for getting them into this mess in the first place.

Bree whomped her pillow with her fist and half wished it was someone real. Maybe that would transfer some of this pain somewhere else instead of trapping it all inside.

Rolling over onto her side, she curled into a ball. Tears trickled down her cheeks, soaking into the slick comforter. It wouldn't be so hard if she could understand what had caused him to call off things in the first place. Maybe then she could accept the decision to no longer be together instead of clinging to unraveled wishes and dreams.

"Why, God?" Bree whispered the words into the quiet room. "Why did you let me fall in love with Nathan if we weren't supposed to be together? Why allow me to get so close to marriage, only to leave me here? Why can't I understand? Why does he think it's good that we're not engaged or married?"

The verses from Sunday's lesson popped into her head. What had they said exactly? Besides all of the wife-submitting-to-the-husband ones, what had Paul wanted spouses to do?

She grabbed her phone and opened her Bible app before doing a search for *husbands*.

"Husbands, love your wives, as Christ loved the church

and gave himself up for her ..." Bree kept scrolling. "In the same way husbands should love their wives as their own bodies. He who loves his wife loves himself."

Hadn't that been how Nathan loved her? Back when he still admitted he did. Because the more time they spent together this week, the more she doubted his story about breaking up with her due to the guys who tagged along on her last girls' trip. There was something more.

It niggled at the edge of her brain, but she couldn't grasp it.

The verses mocked her because before graduation, she would've sworn she and Nathan had that kind of relationship. What happened? What changed?

"As if I'll find answers in this hotel room." Bree got up and started pacing the small space.

The television held no temptation. At this time of day, little would be on worth watching anyway. No telling how long Nathan would be asleep. Sometimes his migraines knocked him out for a whole day. And tomorrow they were supposed to head towards home.

They'd been back at the hotel less than half an hour. The thought of wasting half a day sitting here had her antsy. There had to be something nearby she could explore on her own and then come back and check on Nathan later. He'd never even know she was gone. And it wasn't like she was a kid. She could take care of herself.

Grabbing the keys from the table, she slipped her phone into her purse and headed out. The carriage driver had said something about murals nearby. And her art-loving self wanted to see what he was talking about.

But first, just in case, she'd run down to the corner drugstore she'd seen on the way in. Even though Nathan had said he didn't need anything, maybe they'd have something that could help a bit. An ice pack or something.

Sure enough, she found several items marked as headache relief aides, including a patch that peeled off and cooled a forehead. Maybe she could sneak into his room through their shared door and help a little. Worth a shot, considering the sweet care he'd taken with her the day before.

Back at the hotel, his room was dark, but she could make out his outline on the bed. Looked like he'd simply allowed himself to fall on it and then not moved again. She set the bag of supplies on the bedside table, slipped his glasses off, removed his shoes, and then contemplated what else she might be able to do without waking him. He'd stirred only a bit during all that.

His forehead was wrinkled even while he slept. She gently smoothed it with her fingers like she had in college, and then gently pressed one of the cool patches to the skin. An aroma similar to the vapor rub her mom always used when she had a cold filled the air.

Tracing his face with her gaze, she swallowed hard. If only he'd let her do more—not only with this headache but with whatever had him pushing her away. But there was nothing else she could do until he awoke. Might as well seize what was left of the afternoon and her time in this interesting city.

The last few days, Nathan had made driving through the crazy traffic of Dallas look easy. Behind the wheel with no company but her GPS—a rather saucy British voice—Bree wasn't as confident. She cringed as a horn blared behind her when she slid a lane over.

It hadn't appeared that far from the hotel to the area marked on her map with the most murals. But behind the wheel, it seemed like it was across the whole state of Texas. Shouldn't she have arrived by now?

"You've arrived at your destination." Her GPS sounded smug.

"Thanks a lot. But where do I park?" Bree drove as slowly as she dared, considering the impatient people zipping by her on the four-lane road.

After passing several different lots, each boasting about the same price range, she found a place to make a U-turn and headed back toward the first one. At least this also put her on the correct side of the road, where she wouldn't have to cross traffic again. She gratefully accepted the ticket and pulled into a spot, cutting the engine.

"So much for Texans being friendly." Bree leaned her head against the wheel for a moment. "Not when they're driving."

A tap at her window had her jerking upright. A man dressed in saggy jeans, a tank top, and a ballcap that shaded his face leaned over to peer through the glass. And all her thoughts about being grown up and able to care for herself vanished into thin air.

He motioned her to roll her window down.

Not like he would let her get out until she talked to him. Might as well do it from the car's safety. She cracked the window as little as possible.

"You okay, miss?"

"Yes, fine." She gave a thumbs up. "Just from out of town and needed a minute to recover from your crazy streets."

"Oh, I get it." His laugh echoed off a nearby overpass. "Okay, then. Take care." He sauntered off with several friends.

Bree let out a breath she hadn't realized she'd been holding. She could do this. No big deal. She had maps of Deep Ellum already pulled up on her phone. It shouldn't be that hard to walk around and look at painted walls.

One foot out of the car and a giant raindrop splashed down on her capris.

"Seriously?" Bree glared up at the sky, only to get another few drops in her face.

Okay. Change of plans. Maybe something cool to drink for a few minutes while she waited out this sudden rain shower.

Or some shopping. Her eye caught on a sign for a store that boasted vintage finds at good prices. Perfect.

She dashed through the sporadic raindrops and under the overhang. A bell chimed as she stepped into the shop. The scent of fabric, old perfume, and something else tickled her nostrils as she looked around. Wow.

Dresses, hats, bags. All retro. All chic. All begging to be touched and tried on.

Outside, the rain picked up pace and pounded the sidewalk. Inside, Bree decided she had enough fun here to wait as long as needed. She fingered the silky material of a maroon dress.

"That would look just lovely on you." A clerk smiled from behind another rack. "Let me know if you want to try it on or need help with anything else."

"Thanks so much. I'm mostly just browsing. The rain chased me inside, but I love vintage clothes."

"They're definitely more flattering and pretty than what stores offer now."

"Agreed." Bree touched the lace bodice, wondering if she'd ever need a dress so pretty. She moved away from it with one last loving look. If she were still in school and going to formals, she'd snatch it up in a heartbeat. Especially at that price.

An hour later, she'd examined every fur, tried on several hats, and even drooled over a few pairs of shoes. And she was back to the original dress that had caught her eye. Twisting her lips to the side, she held it up and looked it over again.

"Oh, go try it on, honey. It's still raining, so you might as well have fun, right? And I can knock off ten percent more if it helps."

This clerk spoke Bree's language. Even Nathan couldn't argue against a deal like that. Bree grinned and headed back to the small changing area.

Behind a thick red curtain, she slipped the satiny fabric over her and turned to see her reflection. It was a perfect fit. Not too tight, hitting at the ideal tea length, and completely modest. She had no idea where she'd wear it, but she couldn't resist. If all else failed, maybe she could talk Katie into letting her use it as a bridesmaid dress down the road.

"Okay, I'll take it." Bree slipped out and smiled at the clerk.

"Let's get this wrapped up, then." As the worker carefully folded the garment and slipped it into a bright pink bag, a ray of sunshine beamed through the window.

Obviously, this was meant to be.

"Perfect timing." The clerk passed the bag over the counter and pointed to the weather. "Looks like the rain has passed."

"Yes. On to my original plan."

"What was that?"

"Find something cool to drink, and then go see some of the murals."

She held up a finger. "I have just the thing."

Five minutes later, Bree exited the store into a muggy afternoon. But she couldn't complain. She was now armed with a small map to a great place to get a strawberry lemonade, as well as a few other spots the clerk loved. The puddles on the sidewalk didn't discourage Bree at all.

One slurp of the drink and Bree couldn't quell the smile that filled her face. Just what she needed. She glanced at her phone and followed the directions to the first mural she'd wanted to see.

Colorful wall after colorful wall, Deep Ellum was filled with art and soul. Old warehouses and factories could still be discerned amongst the new builds and revitalization that had taken place over the years. The hum of the interstate was never far away though it was mostly above the little burrow, on overpasses and bridges and ramps.

Bree got lost in the painted walls and didn't pay attention to much else.

Nathan had never had a hangover in his life, but he always imagined waking from a migraine-induced sleep had to be close to the equivalent. Light was still hard to take, a dull ache remained in the recesses of his head, and sudden movements were a no-go.

"Ugh."

He blinked in the stillness and squinted at the clock, trying to figure out how much time he'd lost. Only a few hours. Granted, he still wasn't one hundred percent, but he could probably function on most of his cylinders now, unlike earlier. Maybe Bree would want to find a fun restaurant to end their time in Dallas.

Assuming she was still talking to him.

He ran a hand through his hair and eased into a sitting position, sliding his glasses on his nose. What was on his forehead? He peeled the patch off and blinked at it. Where had this come from?

A bag of other headache helpers sat on the table. Had Bree played nurse while he slept? The idea of her in here, tending to him, shot a zing through his middle.

Smacking his lips, he grimaced. What was it about a migraine that left a cottony feel to his mouth? Upward and onward.

No missed messages on his phone. All was quiet next door. Maybe Bree napped too.

After a quick trip through the bathroom to freshen up a bit, he sent her a text.

No response after five minutes. Hm.

Rapping softly at her connecting door, he frowned. There wasn't much point in waking her if she was resting, but a slight niggle of worry squirmed through his stomach. And after knocking several times, harder with each consecutive failure, he really worried.

"Okay, no big deal. Maybe she's got earbuds in or something." He paced in front of the door, his feet churning up the carpet. "What next?"

Or was she ignoring him? They hadn't exactly ended the morning on a good note. Might not even have started on much of one, not after his awkwardness on the carriage ride. But it had been too close to being romantic, and he'd regretted it as soon as she stepped into the vehicle. That had been fight one for the day.

Then the stupid email, which hadn't even been fully drafted before she threw that fit about Skye or something. And then the migraine. He pressed his palms to his forehead.

It seemed of all the people in the world, he was the best at making a mess out of every single situation.

But even if she was still mad, she couldn't just ignore him forever. They were sharing a car on the way home.

The keys!

He rushed over to where he'd dropped wallet, ChapStick, and room card, but no car keys mingled with the paraphernalia from his pockets.

His heart rate jumped.

Okay. No big deal. Maybe she decided to run out for … something. She'd repeated over and over again how she was a grown-up.

Still …

He punched the button to call. Maybe that would get a reply better than a text. As the ringing continued, he groaned in frustration. Why wasn't she answering?

"Nathan?" She sounded a bit breathless, as if she'd had to run to answer. But her voice also wasn't coming from the other side of the door as well as the receiver, so he knew she wasn't in her room.

"Where are you?" He couldn't help the growl that tinged his question.

"Excuse me?" The way her answer came back, he could picture her with a hand on hip and an eyebrow raised.

"I asked where you are. You didn't answer your door, and the car keys are gone."

"I'm exploring. You didn't sound interested, and you had a migraine, so I figured it was a good time to do this."

"Bree!" He yanked the top of his hair in his hand. "What were you thinking? Do you know how dangerous it is for a woman to walk around by herself in a big city like this?"

She huffed—*huffed!*—into the phone. "Nathan, stop. I'm fine. I'll be back in a little while, okay? I'm glad your head is feeling better."

He pulled the device away from his face and gawked at it. She'd hung up! Not even a goodbye at the end.

"Fine." He pulled his arm back to chunk the useless piece of technology across the room but stopped before actually following through. This thing was too expensive to break over this. Besides, an idea occurred to him.

With a few swipes, Nathan let himself sink into a chair. What his brother lovingly referred to as the "stalker app" was still on his phone, and he'd bet almost anything that Bree hadn't removed him from her approved list. Sure enough, when the app opened, he could click on her lovely face, and it showed him her exact location.

Deep Ellum.

He didn't know much about the area, but if he remembered correctly, the man this morning had mentioned murals there. A few more quick searches on his phone told him more about it. Known for being a melting pot of cultures and arts and music. Yes. He could see her being intrigued by such a place.

But the pictures he saw also didn't look the safest. Not that he could do anything. She'd taken the car.

Unless ...

For the first time in his life, he called a ride share. Now who wasn't being safe in a big city? No turning back now. The driver was on his way.

"God, show me the right way to react in this situation. Because I'm freaking out here." He threw the prayer into the air and then headed down to meet his ride.

Where he had loved how adventurous and fun-loving Bree was in the past, today it held no attraction whatsoever. A man waved at him from a dark blue sedan as he stepped out into the sunlight. He confirmed the information from his phone and climbed in the backseat, hoping he hadn't just entered his very own murder mystery.

The driver looked nice enough as he turned around. "Where we headed?"

"I'm meeting a friend in Deep Ellum." Nathan showed the little dot on his phone where Bree was currently standing. "If you can get me to here, I can find her after that."

"Sure thing." He punched the street name into his phone and pulled out into the traffic zipping by.

For the rest of the world, it was a normal afternoon. The slightly damp streets were full of people going about their everyday lives. But for Nathan, this was the scariest day he'd ever lived.

"You just visiting?" The driver caught his gaze in the mirror.

"Oh, um. Yeah." Was he supposed to admit that to strangers? Wouldn't it just make it more appealing to kill him since no one would know he was here?

Not that the driver knew no one else had a clue where he was.

He'd watched way too many crime shows in the last month. Gripping his phone in his fist, he leaned forward, willing the car to move faster.

"It's a hot time of year to come. Should've waited 'til the fall. Then we have the state fair in town. That's a sight to see." The driver chuckled. "Took my little girl for the first time last year and she couldn't keep her eyes off Big Tex—you know the really big statue of the cowboy?"

"Fun." Nathan squeezed the words past his lips. Surely a man who talked about his little girl like that wasn't a criminal.

"This is the edge of Deep Ellum. Your friend is a couple more streets over. Shouldn't take too long this time of day."

"Thanks." Nathan scanned the streets as they wove through the area, looking for Bree's brown hair. What had she worn that morning? Even if he remembered, she could've changed clothes since then.

No. There she was, just up ahead. He leaned forward and pointed her out to the driver.

With a nod, the guy found a place to pull over and Nathan clicked to pay him. "Thanks so much."

He didn't even wait for a response before shutting the door and all but running toward the reason his stomach was all in knots. Just before he got to her, another man approached from the other direction. Bree's focus was fixed on her phone, and she didn't seem to notice anything around her.

The guy tapped her on the shoulder, causing her head to whip up. But she didn't act nervous or anything despite the man's attire of sagging pants and tank top. Instead, she appeared happy to see him.

Nathan's chest plunged somewhere towards his feet as Bree reached out and touched the guy's arm. His shoes might as well have been glued to the sidewalk. Had she already met someone else in the short amount of time she'd been gone?

14

Deep down, Nathan knew Bree would move on someday. It's what he'd told her to do when he called off their wedding. But it had been only a month. And it wasn't like she'd had much time here in Dallas to get to know anyone. How could she already move on?

And why a guy who looked like that? He might as well have been the complete opposite of Nathan, who always tried to appear neat and put together. Was she rebelling and wanting someone from the opposite side of the spectrum?

The man glanced Nathan's way and straightened as their gazes locked.

Bree turned and her eyes widened. "Nathan?"

His name from her mouth seemed to be what he needed to unlock his legs and be able to move forward once more. He approached even though the man standing beside his ex-fiancée didn't appear to trust him any more than Nathan trusted the stranger. And he couldn't get a read on Bree at all.

"You good?" Tank-top guy asked Bree.

"Yes. Thanks so much for your suggestions." Bree turned a

full-watt smile at the other man. The kind Nathan hadn't seen in months. Another piece of his heart ripped off.

"Have a good afternoon." The man touched the brim of his baseball cap, shot one more wary look Nathan's way, and then headed off to join several other guys on the other side of the street.

"Who was that?" Nathan crossed his arms.

"You know, I didn't even get his name." Bree tilted her head.

"What?" How he kept the question from exploding, he had no idea. It was like Bree wanted to get killed.

"He was checking on me. He'd seen me in the car earlier and made sure I was okay then. And when he spotted me just now, he checked to see if I was feeling better." Bree motioned with a cup of some sort of pinkish liquid.

"Were you not feeling well?" Nathan pressed his hands to her forehead and cheek.

She brushed him aside. "I'm fine. I was just ... dealing with some stuff earlier. Not sick. But what are you doing here?"

"What do you mean, what am I doing here?" He motioned around them at rough-looking brick walls and fire escapes that had seen much better days. "I'm looking for you because you decided to run off to some area we knew nothing about and play the explorer."

"I'm fine, Nathan. I told you that." She crossed her arms, a big pink bag whopping him as she did. "I was just going to walk around a few more blocks and then head back to check on you again. I don't understand why you're freaking out so much about this."

"Did you do stuff like this when you went on girls' trips? Wander around in random places with no one else you knew around so that if anything happened, no one would find you ever again?"

If it were physically possible for eyes to fall out of a head, Bree's would've, she rolled them so hard. "Oh, good grief. No. We almost always did everything together. The only trip where that wasn't true was the last one. And it was Skye who ran off without Katie and me, not the other way around. But I'm fine. Obviously."

"But what if you weren't?"

Bree spun on her heel and started marching the other way, glancing at her phone every now and then, where a map was pulled up.

"You're not even going to answer?" Nathan sped up to catch her.

"Nope."

"Why not?"

"Because it doesn't matter how much I try to explain things to you, you never accept my reasons or answers. And I don't feel like you have the right to demand any answers from me, all things considered."

"What's that supposed to mean?" He almost ran into her when she stopped in front of a wall painted with various men reading newspapers.

After studying it for a minute, she turned to face Nathan. "It means you gave up your right to care about my wellbeing when you decided we shouldn't get married."

He took a step back. Her voice was the coldest he'd ever heard it. And he'd heard her get angry quite a few times back in college. But almost never at him. And never like this.

"Just because I don't think we should get married doesn't mean I can't care about your wellbeing."

"Oh really?" Her eyes glistened as if she were fighting tears. Was she?

"Yes, really. We're still friends. Still have a history together."

"If you cared so much, why did you leave me to clean up the mess of our wedding?" Her lips went in a straight line, and one of her perfectly arched eyebrows raised.

"What do you mean?" He shook his head, wondering if he could get whiplash from a conversation. "Our wedding never happened."

"I know that all too well. I'm the one who had to cancel everything we'd already booked. The venue, the musicians, the cake, the photographer. And some stuff couldn't be returned or reimbursed. You owe my dad several hundred dollars." She poked a finger in his shoulder with that statement and then spun to start walking again.

It had never even dawned on him they might not get their money back for all that stuff. A new churning began in his gut. Had he truly made an even bigger mess by calling things off?

No. He wouldn't buy it. It was still better to be out a few hundred dollars than to be in a marriage that wouldn't work out.

He blinked out of his stupor and almost had to run to catch up to her as she rounded another corner.

"Bree, wait." He caught up with her as she studied another painting—this one much more Texas-themed. "I'm sorry about the money, okay? I didn't think—"

"Did you think anything through?" She cut him off with a glare. "No. You got cold feet and pulled out, and I had to just deal with it. For a month, you didn't answer my calls or texts, didn't reply to emails, nothing. But we're still friends? That's not how friends act. That's how chickens behave."

"Now, wait just a minute." He held up a hand, palm out. "It's not like I don't have good reasons."

"I'm waiting." And she actually tapped her foot while she stood there facing him.

His mouth opened to explain things more, but he couldn't

do it. How could he admit that one phone call from his father had opened his eyes to all sorts of possibilities he hadn't considered before? She wouldn't understand.

"That's what I thought." She turned and headed toward yet another wall.

"Bree."

How much more was she supposed to take? Her heart had broken a dozen times or more over the last few days. And every time she thought things couldn't get worse, they did.

Here he was, acting like he wanted to take care of her. But if he did, wouldn't he have made her his wife four days before? Then she would've let him take care of her for the rest of their lives.

As she approached the next mural, she immediately regretted it. Huge tears appeared to fall from the eyes painted on the brick, bringing moisture to her own. And if there was one thing she didn't want to show Nathan right now, it was tears.

"Is that wall crying?" Nathan puffed up beside her. "Why would anyone want to see a wall that's crying?"

Bree swiped at the moisture gathering under her own lashes.

"Wait. Are *you* crying?" Nathan pressed a palm to his forehead for a moment. "Please, don't, Bree. You know I hate it when you cry."

Of all the—

"Well, I'd hate to make you uncomfortable!" Bree flopped her hands at her sides. "Heaven forbid you have to admit you broke my heart!"

The words escaped before she could snatch them back. But

between the tears and everything else, she couldn't read his expression. So much for him not knowing how much she hurt —all thanks to him.

She turned her back to him. If only she could see well enough to walk farther away. Oh, to be back in the hotel room where she'd have the privacy needed for a full-out sob session! But no. This had to happen in the middle of Deep Ellum, where her delightful afternoon had turned darker than the clouds from earlier.

"Bree." Nathan's deep voice held sorrow, too, and his hand on her shoulder was gentle.

"Please, stop." She choked the words out. "Haven't you done enough?"

"I don't know how to make it better."

A sob shuddered through her body. "I'm not sure you can anymore."

"Here's a table over in this alcove. Let's go sit down for a minute." He steered her out of the sun-drenched parking lot and over to an area outside a little restaurant. No one was out in the heat of the afternoon, so it allowed a bit more privacy.

Bree dug through her bag, hoping she'd remembered to include some tissues in its dark depths. Of course not. Nathan jumped up and walked away, and she almost gave in to the scream wanting to escape her lungs. Where was he going now?

He returned a moment later, hands full of napkins and a sheepish expression on his face. "Would these help?"

She accepted a few and mopped at the moisture clinging to her cheeks and dripping from her chin.

"Can you tell me what brought this on?"

When she shot him a look, he waved and shook his head.

"I mean, besides us not being married."

Pressing a napkin to both eyes, she hoped the pressure would convince the ducts to dry it up already. Of course that didn't work. How could she explain to Nathan the torment this week had been?

A slurp of her now watered-down lemonade bought her another moment. "Let's see. You decided to spend the week with me despite us not having to since the cruise was canceled."

He opened his mouth, but she held up a finger.

"Then you challenged me to prove my trustworthiness by showing you what it was like on my other road trips to prove I never wanted to cheat on you. Although, let's be honest. There's no way this road trip has been anything like any of my others because the girls aren't here and it's a different location. And the man who decided to tag along has known me for the last three years."

He pinched his lips together but didn't reply.

"Also, I don't think you ever really thought I cheated on you. I think you were looking for an excuse." She shook her head. "But that's beside the point."

Still he had no answer.

"Since we've been here, you have shown me every side of you except the real one. I only get that one in glimpses. I never know what to expect. I thought I saw the old you Saturday evening when we ate pizza, but then he disappeared again. He showed up for a few minutes at the farmer's market. And at the museum. And the Arboretum, for that matter. Then, when you were so worried about me when I got sick, I hoped maybe things might get back to normal."

"Normal." He chuffed and looked off towards the crying wall instead of at her.

She decided to ignore that and continued her earlier thoughts. "So, when you suggested the carriage ride, I half expected it to be as romantic as it looked. But you were stiffer than an ice statue, an amazing feat considering how hot it is here. At the park, when you showed me up at ping pong, I saw the old you. But then he hid behind his money and numbers, and I guess our fight brought on your migraine."

She glanced at him, but he still refused to look her way.

"Needless to say, when you showed up here, half-panicked over my wellbeing, is it any wonder I'm confused? I can't figure out why you're so worried about me because you keep telling me you don't want me in your life. You can't have it both ways, Nathan. Either you care or you don't care."

Her voice had risen through the diatribe, and several people glanced their way as they walked past on the sidewalk, but she pretended she didn't notice. This needed to happen, and if they had it out here in the open, at least the hotel wouldn't kick them out for disturbing the peace. Besides, she was tired of walking on eggshells around Nathan, unsure which side of him he'd display.

"Are you done?" His Adam's apple bobbed, and he finally brought his steel-gray eyes into her line of sight.

"I don't know." From yelling to just above a whisper in one minute. But that's all the energy she had left.

"Why is it so hard for you to believe that I still care about you even though I don't think we ought to get married?"

"Are you even listening to yourself?" And there came the stupid tears again. "Do you hear the words coming out of your mouth? They don't even make sense!"

"Of course they do." He leaned forward, his forearms on the table. "If you love someone, you're supposed to let her go."

"You did not just quote whatever that is!" She slapped her palms on top of the iron table. "Because that is the stupidest thing I've ever heard. If two people love each other, they're supposed to do something about it. Like get married. Not throw it away."

"I didn't throw anything away." He leaned forward even more. "I was trying to protect you."

"Protect me from what?" She scooted closer. "From you?"

"Exactly!" He jutted out his chin. "I'm no good for you."

"Well, that's ridiculous. And I'm obviously not doing so hot without you either." Her face was only about an inch from his, the closest it had come since the day he called everything off.

His breath fanned her skin as he exhaled, and it came out rather shaky. His eyes darted between hers and then lowered towards her lips. What would happen if she closed the slight distance? Would he run away? Would he melt back into the man she loved?

"Y'all are in the wrong spot." A man's voice jerked her back to reality, and she banged into the arm of her chair.

"What?"

"The mural you're wanting is a few more blocks that way." He pointed, his face jovial as he glanced between her and Nathan.

"We'll go check it out. Thanks." She quickly pushed away from the table and Nathan followed suit.

He was quiet as they meandered past several more murals. Which was the one the man had meant? And then she froze.

A staircase worked its way up the side of the building, and following its ascent was a big plus sign, an equal sign, and a giant heart. It was obvious two people were supposed to stand on either side of the addition symbol to make up the equation. And a few months back, she would have blissfully jumped into position, dragging Nathan with her and begging someone to snap the shot.

Her fingers reached out automatically and wove through his. Instead of pulling away like she'd expected him to, he tightened the grip. And it was like coming home.

"Need someone to take your picture?" A voice from behind them pulled her thoughts back to the present.

"Oh, that's okay—"

But her excuses were cut short when Nathan nudged her. "Why not?"

So many reasons. For one, everything still unsaid between the two of them. For another, well ... actually, the first pretty much summed up all the others.

"Here. Go get in position, and I'll snap it really quick for you." The stranger smiled and held out her hand for Bree's phone.

"Um." Bree quickly switched from the map to her camera app before handing over the device and following Nathan to the stairs.

No telling what her face looked like. She set her bags down at the bottom where they'd hopefully be out of the frame, then stepped up past Nathan. He squeezed her arm on the way. If only she could get a peek, a glimpse of what was going through his head right now. She wouldn't even ask for the full picture.

"Ready?" The girl smiled and gave them a thumbs up. "Say Dallas!"

Bree glanced at Nathan and found him looking back at her.

"Aww. That was so cute. Now, how about one looking this way?"

Bree couldn't help the grin that spread. The girl's accent was twangy and fit in so well with their surroundings. And a bit of hope wound its way through the cracks and crevices of her aching chest. Could she hold on to it?

Or would it slip away again the moment they stepped off this staircase?

15

The walk back towards the car was quiet. The afternoon had passed its apex, and the people out and about weren't staying in the sun for long. A million thoughts ran sprints through Bree's head.

Why had Nathan agreed to that picture? Had it been the almost kiss?

That had been an almost kiss, hadn't it? When they'd gotten so close. Without thinking, she reached up and touched her lips.

"Some of these murals are strange, huh?" Nathan's question had her yanking her hand back down again, hoping he hadn't noticed.

"Not my style, for sure." She tugged on his sleeve. "Oh, look at that one. I guess I missed it coming the other way."

The wall stretched out with various Dallas and Texas icons and landmarks, the letters of the city stretching high amidst the chaos. She glanced both ways and then dashed across the road to see it closer. She might like this even more than the ornament she'd bought a few days before.

"I think this one is my favorite of all the ones I've seen." She tilted her head back to see to the top of Reunion Tower.

"Even more than …?"

… Than the staircase one. She knew exactly what he started to ask. And the wistful look that crossed his face when he looked back in that direction had her wondering about more.

"Maybe. This one just makes me happy because of the colors and crazy way it's all out of proportion." She thrust her phone at him. "Here. Take my picture."

"What? Again? Why?"

"Let's just say it's what we do on road trips. Skye was forever finding something fun for us to stand in front of and take a photo."

She ignored his eyeroll and posed near the middle of the mural. He shook his head. But he lifted the phone and took the picture.

"Here." He held it back out to her.

"Thanks." Shielding the screen with her other hand, she scrolled back through the snaps he'd taken. Cute. "Want me to do yours?"

"I'm not really a stand-in-front-of-a-painting-and-take-a-picture kind of guy." He stared into the distance as if afraid she'd ask why he volunteered to do just that not fifteen minutes before.

She was tempted, but she held her tongue. "If you prefer, I saw one earlier that had aliens with the abduction beam coming down. We could put you in front of it."

"Hoping they'll take me far, far away?" He finally let his line of sight return to her and the impact made her catch her breath.

"Nope. I need you to drive back to the hotel. Getting over here was not a fun experience."

"I don't even want to know what that means." He shook

his head and then studied the wall one more time. "Wonder what the deal is with the big eyeball."

Following the direction his finger indicated, she tilted her head when she noticed the faceless eyeball for the first time. "Huh. No idea. Maybe it's just one of those random things the artist includes that has nothing to do with the rest of the painting."

He shrugged and then motioned toward the sidewalk again. "Ready to head back and get out of this heat for a while?"

"More than." She clutched her shopping bag to her chest as they walked. "How's your head, by the way? This didn't make things worse, did it?"

"Still a bit of an ache. And things are off enough I know I had one earlier." He held his hands out as if weighing something. "But if it wasn't much better, I wouldn't be standing here right now. Thanks for the patch, by the way."

"Oh, um ... you're welcome." Her cheeks warmed as she remembered sneaking into his room earlier. "It must've helped. It surprised me when you showed up this afternoon. I remember some of the ones in college lasting most of the day."

He cringed as if reliving parts of those. "They're mostly stress-triggered. Though when I stepped outside and saw the puddles, I wondered if this wasn't a bit weather related, too."

"How did you even get here, by the way? I meant to ask earlier and got ... sidetracked."

"I called a rideshare."

Her feet froze. He'd used a service he declared one of the stupidest ways to die? Because he'd been worried about her?

Nathan turned from where he'd kept going when she stopped. "What?"

Shaking her head, she returned to his side.

"Where did you park the car?"

Their arms bumped, pinkies twisting together. His latched on a bit tighter, and she found she couldn't complain, although it brought up even more questions. This was one of the first ways they'd held hands in the beginning. As if only holding pinkies would be less conspicuous.

"It should be just up ahead." She motioned with her other hand, trying to still the extra flutters going through her insides.

Do not make a big deal out of this. Don't jinx it. Do you even want to go back down this road? After all he's put you through?

"Should be?"

"It's there." Pointing it out, she smirked. "See? I'm not completely helpless."

"And yet, you want me to drive."

"Please and thank you."

He stood waiting, as if she was supposed to say something else. "I'll need the keys."

"Oh! Right." Her cheeks heated as she remembered threatening to dig them out of his pocket earlier, and she quickly pulled them from her purse. "Here you go."

"Thanks." He opened her door and waited until she was seated before going around and starting the ignition. "Let's go."

As he wound through streets that began to look a bit familiar in places, something crazy caught her eye. She leaned forward and pointed. "What is that?"

"What?"

"See if you can get over somewhere around there. I want to investigate and see if that is what I think it is."

"What, Bree?"

"A giant eyeball!"

"Really?" He sounded skeptical, though whether about the object or her desire to see it, she couldn't tell. Still, he wove his way around and found a parking place not too far away.

They walked together up to the giant sculpture, and Bree couldn't shake the feeling it was watching them. It towered over them in a small courtyard surrounded by an iron fence. Still, the details were easy to make out from the sidewalk.

"That thing has to be thirty feet tall." Nathan craned his head back to look up at the top.

"This is insane. I have to take a picture with it to send to Skye. She'd freak over this."

"You and Skye are crazy."

"Maybe so, but I'm taking a picture anyway." She tugged at his arm. "Get in here."

Phone flipped to do a selfie, Bree made a face with wide eyes at the camera, the giant eyeball staring over her shoulder. "Come on, Nathan. Make your eyes really wide like mine."

"Sorry. I'm new to this whole selfie thing." He grumbled, but his blue-greys grew larger, and she snapped it before he could change his mind.

"I'm going to win you over yet."

He mumbled something, and she couldn't be certain, but it sounded a lot like, "You might already have."

She pinched her lips together, tucking that away, and sauntered back toward the car.

"This way, Bree." Nathan pointed over his shoulder.

"But we parked over here." She indicated the other direction.

"No." He grabbed her hand and pulled. "This way."

And sure enough, a minute later, there was their car.

"Okay, you win."

"Can we go back now?" He turned the ignition.

"Yes." She smiled as she texted the photo to Skye. She was going to flip.

Nathan was of two minds. One was beating him as hard and fast as possible, calling him any number of names his mama wouldn't approve. The other was cheering and encouraging him to continue back down the road he'd somehow veered onto this afternoon with Bree—though chiding him for not grabbing that kiss while he had the chance.

What was he doing?

She hummed happily in the seat beside him, back to the carefree, joyous girl he'd fallen in love with all those years ago. All because of a few pictures and some handholding. But was he misleading her?

He didn't want to be. No way on earth did he want to break her heart any more than he already had. And for the first time, he realized that his own heart wasn't the only one broken when he'd called things off.

In trying to protect her, he'd inflicted pain.

"You're awful quiet over there." Bree cut into the silence, stirring his thoughts around into an ever-muddying pool of sludge.

"Thinking. And trying to make sure I pay attention to the other drivers."

"They're nuts around here. And that's saying something, considering I've been living in Memphis with Katie."

"Nashville can be crazy too." He drummed his fingers on the steering wheel as he waited for a light to change.

"I remember from the few times I was over there with you." And there went her voice dipping into the sadness again. He couldn't win for losing tonight.

"Right." He hit the turn signal and shifted into another lane. "I guess I forgot you'd been there that much."

"You forgot apartment shopping with me? Registering for all those wedding gifts? Some of them I still have to return."

A fist to the jaw would hurt less than the reality of all she'd had to deal with in the last month. A disaster he'd left for her to clean up, not thinking ... Well, not thinking just about summed it up completely, didn't it? Had he used his brain at all in the last two months? Since Dad called ...

"Anyway, I'm just glad your head is better enough that you can drive us back." She reached over and squeezed his arm.

Warmth spread from his elbow up through his shoulder and filled his chest cavity. Just from one little touch. If they'd not gotten interrupted earlier, would he have worked up the courage to kiss her? And where would that leave them now?

Ahead, Reunion Tower rose above most of the rest of the skyline of downtown Dallas. The huge globe at the top intrigued him and terrified him at the same time. But Bree would love getting to go up there.

He glanced at her out of the corner of his eye, but she stared at something outside the car.

The restaurant probably wouldn't even be able to fit in another reservation this late in the day. So, why did his heart rate pick up speed and sweat form on his palms?

Because the more he contemplated the idea, the more it became clear that it would be the perfect ending to their stay in Dallas. That's why. And because Bree would go absolutely ga-ga for it.

He glanced at the clock. Almost five. No way would there still be a reservation available.

In the parking garage, he found a spot as close to the elevators as possible. They walked through the lobby and rode the elevator up as if nothing had happened between the two of them this afternoon to change things. As if his whole axis hadn't tilted, spinning his world out of control.

She paused outside her door. "Want to clean up and grab some dinner?"

"Yeah. I may do some research and see what sounds good nearby."

Her eyes widened, and she slipped her sunglasses up on top of her head. "Really?"

"Last night in Dallas, right? Might as well find something to remember."

"As long as it's not as memorable as the Chinese place we ate at yesterday." She wrinkled her pert little nose, and it took all his willpower not to lean down and press a kiss to the tip.

"Got it. No Chinese."

"Just let me know what kind of place we're heading to." She held up the pink bag. "I do have a new dress just dying to get out."

"Well, we can't have that, can we?" His lips twitched. "I'll let you know."

He waited until her door clicked closed and then entered his own room. Pushing the connecting door shut the rest of the way, he paused. Part of him was afraid the connection they'd made this afternoon would sever if he shut this barrier. But he also didn't want her to be able to hear anything he said on the phone, either.

With a few swipes and some quick typing, he found the information he needed. Hesitating only a second, he pushed to call the restaurant. The phone rang three times, and then a friendly voice answered.

"Um, yes." He stumbled, fighting for the words needed. "I don't suppose you'd still have a reservation available for this evening?"

"Let's see what we have. How many would be in the party?"

"Just two." And Bree's new dress, apparently.

"Would seven work?"

"I'll take it. Do you know if we could come up to the observation deck earlier?"

"I'll make a note of it now. What name should I put it under?"

"Hart. Nathan Hart."

"I've got you down for a table for two at seven o'clock this evening, Mr. Heart. We'll see you then."

"Yes." He somehow choked the word out before hanging up.

What had he just signed himself up for? Did he really just agree to go up in a super-high tower that looked down over the city of Dallas? He covered his mouth as a gag worked its way up his throat.

Find anything?

Bree texted.

He squeezed his eyes closed for a moment and then answered.

How fancy is your new dress?

Not too fancy, but fancy enough.

Her sass came through the text loud and clear.

Put it on. We have reservations for seven but something else around six.

The dots bounced forever on her end, and he waited to see what kind of reply he'd get.

Really?

Really. I'll pick you up around five-forty.

Nathan Hart, you are a first-class idiot and a jerk. What are you doing to this girl?

Then the squeal came through the hotel wall, and his stomach flipped for a whole new reason. This would be worth it. For her.

Now to get himself ready. What had he packed for the cruise that would work in a pinch? He had the outfit for the fancy dinner, but he didn't want to wear a tux.

Maybe ...

16

Josh's text buzzed through on the phone on the bathroom counter as Nathan tried to shave his face more quickly than was smart.

> When did you decide to come home?

> We're headed back tomorrow. Why?

> Does Mom know you and Bree spent the week together?

Nathan narrowed his eyes and pushed to call his brother instead of texting a reply. "Why?"

"Why what?" Josh's voice came through the speaker phone, sounding falsely innocent.

"Why are you asking if Mom knows I spent the last few days with Bree?" Nathan rinsed out his razor and toweled his cheeks.

"Look, I talked to Katie today. She said Bree sounded sort of upset this morning. So, I thought I would check in. And since

Mom's right on the way home from Dallas, and you said you were driving, I wondered if you were going to stop in and see her."

Nathan carried the device back to the other room and tossed it on the bed while he slipped into his button-up shirt. "I wasn't planning on it. I mean, we do have to return the rental car by a certain day, you know."

"Mm. I'm sure that was in your figuring when you planned all this out." Josh's voice sounded less than convinced.

"Look, you checked in." Nathan fastened his belt and then rolled his sleeves. "Two nights in a row. Consider yourself off the hook for whatever it is you think you're doing. We can talk more when I get home, if I still claim you as a relative then."

"What are you doing?"

"What do you mean, what am I doing? I'm getting ready to go eat dinner." Nathan paused as he patted some aftershave on his face. What was he doing? He hadn't gotten this dressed up in ages—barely even wore a polo and khakis to church services anymore.

"Go eat dinner where?"

"None of your business, actually." He slipped his wallet into his back pocket and glanced at the clock—time to wrap up this nuisance of a phone call.

"You're going with Bree?"

"Yes. I'll eat dinner with Bree. Just like I have for the last few nights. Because somehow, our friends and family decided it would be fun to set us up and send us on a trip that a hurricane canceled."

"Don't break her heart again, Big Brother." Josh's voice was the most serious he'd ever heard it.

"I never wanted to in the first place." Nathan turned off the speaker and pressed the phone to his ear. "But maybe you should've worried more about that before you decided it would be a good idea to trick us into taking a trip together."

He didn't even wait for his brother's response. Instead, he hung up before Josh could chide him for the flippant remark. Maybe Bree was right. Maybe he was a chicken.

Studying his reflection in the mirror, he scowled. He'd need a haircut in the next few weeks. Some of the waves seemed to have a mind of their own, going any direction but the one he'd combed them. Bags still hung under his eyes where he'd fought off most of the migraine earlier.

What would Bree see when she looked at him? He'd never understood how she found him attractive in the first place. But she had. How many times had she told him his hair was the softest she'd ever felt? Or that she loved the color of his eyes?

They were just blue. Not even the stunning aquamarine of hers. His tended more toward grey.

He squinted at his reflection and pursed his lips. Was Josh right to worry? Maybe he should just drop Bree off and let her experience this by herself.

As if that had gone over well that morning.

No way.

The time on his phone changed, and he glanced down. A minute later than he'd promised to pick her up. Ready or not, time to go.

Grabbing the car keys, he headed out and gently knocked on her door. One way or another, tonight would be a night to remember.

***

Bree smoothed down the fabric of her dress. Only a few wrinkles had worked their way into the fabric in the bag this afternoon. She'd been able to release most of them by running a steamy shower in the bathroom while she fixed her hair at the sink. Was it too much? Maybe she should change into the dress she wore Sunday.

It had been so easy to send back the flirty text earlier, but now that things were real, she second-guessed herself. Was this a date? Dinner between friends? Something else that had no real title because they were making it up as they went along?

She tugged a wave that seemed determined to flip out at the end and spoke to her reflection. "Why does it matter, Bree? He's the one who called it off. Not you."

But he was also the one she still pictured in her dreams when she thought about the future.

The rap at the door pulled her from her worries and contemplations. No time like the present. Grabbing her smaller purse, she took a deep breath and pulled open the door.

Nathan waited in the hallway, his hands twisted together as if he were as nervous as she was. His light blue oxford shirt fit just right, and the rolled sleeves showed off arms more muscular than she remembered. The slacks were a dark grey, almost black. And he'd obviously just shaved because a tiny bit of shaving cream clung near his ear.

"Hi."

His eyes grew wider as they took in her dress and hair. Appreciation ... and maybe something else ... warmed up the silver and brought out more blue. She hadn't seen that look in a while.

"Is this okay?" She spun in a circle, allowing the A-line skirt to flare out a bit.

"You're beautiful."

A lump formed in her throat. How long had it been since he'd said that to her? Too long. Was it something he meant or habit after all their years together?

"Bree." He caught her hand in one of his. "I mean it. You're gorgeous."

She sniffed and forced a smile, putting on a persona more lighthearted than she felt. "Oh, this old thing? I found it today when I was waiting out the rainstorm. No big deal."

"You make it a big deal. It's perfect on you." He gave her a little tug. "Ready to go?"

She nodded, unable to speak after that. Was this real? Had a miracle happened this afternoon and she somehow missed seeing the bright light from heaven?

He escorted her through the door and down the hallway, his hand hovering at the small of her back. Some girls might find it condescending or too old-fashioned, but it made her feel cherished and safe. And when he opened her door for her, she decided she never wanted to be a liberated woman. This was much nicer.

"So, do I get a hint of where we're going?" She studied the area as they drove through the heart of the city.

"A hint, huh?" He cut his eyes her way. "Let's just say that tonight, I decided the sky was the limit."

"The sky's the limit ..." Leaning forward, she skimmed the skyline, tracing over various buildings until she spotted one round on top. No. He wouldn't have booked them at the Reunion Tower, would he?

"You okay over there?"

The car headed right toward it. Had he really? She fixed him with a stare. Who was this man seated next to her?

"Bree?"

"Did you really? After all that talk about things costing too much? Up there?" She pointed at the tower immediately in front of them now.

"Well, Dallas doesn't have an Empire State building, but this place is 470 feet up. I figured it would work as a stand-in."

She blinked several times as he parked and walked around the vehicle to open her door. "You're serious? Nathan, this is amazing. But we're just going up to look and then eating somewhere else, right? That's why we left so early?"

"Nope. I got us into the restaurant too."

Bree squeezed his arm, muffling her squeal of delight in his sleeve. "For real?"

"For real." He glanced to the top. "Ready to go up?"

"Yes." She followed the direction he looked. "But you're afraid of heights."

He swallowed so hard she wondered how his Adam's apple didn't go down with it. "I am."

"Why on earth would you book something like this—especially considering the price—if you're terrified of being almost five hundred feet in the air?"

"For you." He said it as if it were the most obvious thing in the world. And two months before, it would have been, but tonight?

"Also, I was assured that it's completely safe, there are tons of bars to keep people from falling, and it was the closest thing I could get to what you wanted." He shrugged. "Besides, this is much shorter than the Empire State Building, and cheaper too."

"You have to pay to go to the observation deck there?" She hadn't known that.

"Everywhere. Anywhere a man can make a buck, he will." He gave a single nod. "Okay, let's get this over with."

The elevator had glass around it so they could see the view as they rose. Amazing for her, but not so much for Nathan. He was quiet as they made their way up, and his pulse beat erratically under her finger. Torturing himself ... for her. It had her feeling like the most special woman in the world. But was it worth it?

"Okay. We have a little under an hour up here on the observation deck, and then we'll head on to the restaurant." His voice had a bit of a tremor to it.

She wrapped her arm around his waist and held him as tightly as she could as they stepped out of the elevator. Her breath whooshed out of her as she caught the view through the windows. The floor slowly turned, giving them a different view inch by inch. Dallas spread out before them, the cars below tiny little ants crawling down the interstates.

"Wow." It took a tug or two, but she got him moving closer to the edge.

Screens were set at intervals, along with telescopes and other instruments to help people see better and learn more about what was below. She touched a screen, and it gave her information about the building in front of them. Nifty.

"Oh, look, Nathan. Is that the park we went to this morning?"

He didn't say anything.

She glanced away from the vista and fear shot through her. Nathan's skin was paler than normal—almost translucent. His eyes never wavered from looking straight ahead as if should he happen to lower them at all, he'd pass out completely.

"Nathan." She steered him back to a bench closer to the center of the tower. "Hey, babe. Can you look at me?"

His eyes slowly focused on her. "It's really high."

"Right. We talked about that. But we're safe. See all the bars? There's no way we could fall from here. None. Maybe try to focus on finding the places we've already been?"

He swallowed and then nodded.

"Okay?" She rose and then helped him stand again too. "Here we go."

Back at the edge, the park was slightly farther to the right now, and other places were centered before them. "There's where JFK was shot."

As they continued to slowly revolve and see more and more landmarks appear, he relaxed a bit. He was even able to smile when an attendant came and took their picture. His skin was back to normal and his breathing regular by the time they headed to the five-star restaurant.

"The reservation should be under Hart." Nathan stood straight while the hostess checked her list.

"Yes, here it is."

Bree glanced and saw that it had been spelled like the organ. She quickly covered a grin. He probably got that all the time, but it seemed fitting tonight, all things considered.

The eatery had to be the poshest place she'd ever been. Golden lights and modern furniture. Shiny and sleek, and all she could think about was how expensive it must be. Had Nathan been abducted by aliens and sent back a different person?

Bree glanced over the menu as the skyline continued to go by outside her window. Everything was beautiful, but it also came with a price. And she began to worry Nathan had lost his mind. She glanced over at him.

"Order what you want." It sounded mostly normal, but she could tell his jaw was tighter than usual.

She laid her menu down and reached over to cover his hand. "I can help."

"What?"

"I can cover my own meal tonight. I've worked a little this week, teaching online. And I can do more when I get back. This is too much." Besides, if he paid, it really would be a date— probably the most romantic one she'd ever been on. And she was terrified that at the end, everything would disappear and go back to normal.

"You did help. You kept me from having a panic attack earlier." He sent her a grin and then returned to studying the menu. His finger had been following the end with the price tags, but he lifted it and knocked on the table. "I'm getting a steak."

"That sounds good. But this salmon looks divine." She tapped a picture on her own menu.

"Go for it."

"Are you sure you didn't hit your head on something earlier today?" Bree's question pulled him from studying the layout of the interstates below.

"What are you talking about?" He frowned.

"All this. Ever since ..." This was harder than she'd expected it to be. "Ever since this afternoon, after ... after we sat at that table. Well, you've just been acting different than you were before. More like the old you. Except for the spending money part."

A corner of his lips turned up at that last statement. "Can't a guy want to make the last night in a city special?"

It was hard not to notice that he left off saying anything about her. "Sure. I guess so."

"Besides, this is sort of like giving us book ends. We started our time here eating at a New York-style pizza place. And this is probably the closest Dallas has to offer for the Empire State Building. I figured it would complete the experience."

She pinched her lips together to keep from laughing. He had no idea what her idea of an Empire State Building experience was. Because in her dreams, she kissed the man she loved at the very top. And while this evening was rather romantic, she hadn't noticed any more hints of a kiss.

Which was a bit of a shame.

17

"Hi. I'm Marcus, and I'll be taking care of you this evening." An impeccably dressed man stood next to their table, black notebook in hand. "What can I get you started on tonight? We have quite a few nice wines."

Bree blushed. For so long, she'd wanted to be considered an adult, but now that she was here, it was more awkward than satisfying. Nathan passed the notebook full of alcoholic choices back to Marcus with a shake of his head.

"Just water for me."

Bree gave a nod when the waiter turned her way. "Yes. That sounds perfect."

"All right. And would you like me to bring you an appetizer while you wait for your food?" Marcus looked between them as if expecting this would be his cheap table for the night.

"I think we'll just wait for the main course." Nathan gave a semi-smile to the waiter.

"Right. I'll be right back with those drinks." Marcus tapped his notebook against the drink menu, gave a swift nod, and then headed toward the bar.

"Think he regrets having our table?" Bree couldn't help the giggle that escaped.

"Why would he? It's not like we're only ordering water."

Bree shook her head and let her gaze wander once more to the world below them. "Never mind."

Marcus returned with their waters and scribbled down their meal requests. "I'll have that right out."

"Aren't you getting a bit dizzy, staring out the window like that?" Nathan pulled her attention back to him.

"No. We're spinning slowly enough that it's not bothering me at all, actually." She motioned around them. "This is really nice. Thank you."

"For what?"

"For making sure I had this experience. Because of tonight, this might just be my favorite road trip ever."

He raised an eyebrow. "That's saying a lot considering how many rough moments we had over the last few days."

"I'll admit things didn't go completely as planned." A smirk took over her lips. "If they had, we'd be sitting on a boat right now."

"A ship." The twinkle in his eyes lightened the correction. "True. I guess none of your other trips had quite as many blunders at the beginning, huh?"

"Maybe not. Though, there was that one trip where two random guys followed us around thanks to Skye inviting them. And Camden's attraction to Katie."

Nathan stiffened, though maybe not as much as he had at the beginning of the week. "I guess that would change your plans a bit, huh?"

"A bit." She ran her finger over the condensation on the side of her glass. "Though I think they just made me miss my fiancé more. Because I felt a bit like a fifth wheel."

Nathan's head jerked up, and he studied her.

"Of course, I also knew I'd be taking a trip with my fiancé a month later and that I'd get him all to myself." Lifting a shoulder, she dared to glance his way before looking back down at her silverware. "At least, that was the plan."

He didn't say anything. But before the silence could get awkward, their food arrived and the amazing aromas wafting up from the plates gave them something else to focus on. She stretched her hands across and wove her fingers through his.

A grin twitched around the edges of his mouth. "I take it you're ready to pray."

"The sooner we pray, the sooner we can dig in."

"Noted." He bowed his head, and she followed suit. "Lord, we thank You. Thank You for this beautiful day, for the time spent together. Thank You for our friends and family who love us so much and want what's best for us. Thank You for this food."

He paused so long she wondered if she'd just missed the amen, but his head was still bowed.

"And thank You for this woman across from me. Lord, I don't deserve her." He squeezed her fingers and rose from the table, heading towards the restrooms.

She blinked a few times to try to curtail some of the moisture gathering in her eyes. Should she wait for him to come back? The dish invited her to dig in. Maybe she'd just wait a minute or two.

"Everything okay?" Marcus appeared at her side.

"It looks great." She pointed to the empty chair across from her. "He had to run to the restroom for a minute."

"Let me know if there's anything else I can get for you." Marcus nodded and moved to another table.

Another employee stopped to show a printout of the photo they'd had taken earlier. It was good. He listed the prices, and she bit back the desire to haggle. Nathan would tell her it wasn't worth it, but the smiles on both their faces had her itching to keep the memory anyway.

She removed the quoted amount from her purse and replaced it with the photographic evidence there was something still between them, whether Nathan admitted it or not.

Just when Bree was going to give up and eat without him, Nathan slid back into his seat. His eyelashes were damp, but other than that, he just looked like the same handsome guy who'd come in with her. He lifted his knife and fork in salute, and she let his disappearance slide. Were they making progress or backsliding?

Everything about the food was perfect, the salmon breaking apart and almost melting on her tongue. The rice was well-seasoned, and the veggies tender. She nibbled a roll as Nathan finished off his steak. He caught her staring, and her cheeks heated.

"What?" He swiped his napkin over his mouth.

"I don't know." She set her plate aside. "Was it good?"

"It was."

"Worth it, then?"

"Not something I'd do every day, but nice for a special occasion." Crossing his fork and knife on his plate, he leaned back in his chair.

Marcus stepped up to their table once more. "How was everything?"

"It was great. Thanks so much." Bree took a sip of water.

"And are you interested in any dessert tonight?"

Nathan started to shake his head, but Bree wasn't letting him off that easy.

"What are the options tonight?"

"We have a chocolate brownie sundae, a cherry cobbler, and a limoncello cake as the main options." Marcus waited, their plates balanced in his hands.

"Oh, Nathan. You love lemon. What if we do that one? I'll pay for the dessert, and we can split it."

Nathan opened his mouth and then closed it again before waving his hand her direction. "Order what you want. But I'm pretty full. You may have to finish it off yourself."

With a grin, Bree held up a finger to Marcus. "One piece of the lemon cake and two forks, please. And two cups of coffee."

"We'll be up all night." Nathan did protest that time.

"Decaf?" Bree glanced at the waiter.

He nodded. "I'll have it right out."

"You know I'm not letting you pay for that, right?"

"You will if I pull out my card before you do." She lifted a brow.

"We'll see about that." Nathan's phone began to ring, and he quickly pulled it out and silenced it, a frown wrinkling his forehead. "It's my mom."

"Do you need to take it?"

He shook his head. "I'll call her back in a little while."

But his phone began to ring again, almost immediately. He pressed the deny button and then quickly typed out a message. Bree leaned forward.

"If you need to go talk to her, you can."

"It can wait a few minutes. At least until after your dessert."

She moved out of the way so Marcus could set the decadent confection in front of her. The aroma of the coffee had her inhaling deeply. Just what she needed.

After only one bite, she groaned. "Oh my goodness. You have to try this."

Nathan started to protest, but she held a forkful out to him and lifted a brow. Obligingly he leaned forward and let her slip it between his lips. A moan followed as his eyes slipped shut.

"Right?" She took another bite for herself. "Now are you glad I ordered it?"

"It's really good."

"Makes you rethink all our wedding cake choices, huh?" The words left her mouth before she even realized what she was saying.

The mention of their wedding didn't hurt quite as much this time as it had before. Maybe bringing it up so much over the last few days had helped get him used to thinking about it. Or maybe he was just emotionally numb.

"I don't know." Nathan savored a bite before putting her completely out of her misery. "You can't go wrong with chocolate."

"True." She drew the word out before inching another bite off her fork and into her mouth. It was mesmerizing, watching the confection slip between her lips. Lips he'd almost kissed earlier that afternoon.

His phone chimed with a message. Mom.

Call me when you're done with dinner. I have a question.

He couldn't remember the last time she'd worked so hard to get him on the phone. She usually left a message and accepted that he'd call when he got the chance. Tonight she'd called as though it were an emergency—though the text didn't sound urgent. Something strange was going on.

"Everything still good over here?" Marcus laid the checks on the table facedown, almost halfway between Nathan and Bree.

"It's great." Nathan covered the tabs before Bree could even start to reach for them. "I'll take care of this."

"At your convenience."

Nathan handed him his debit card along with both receipts.

"I was supposed to pay for dessert." Bree pursed her lips into a pout.

"I've got it. You're still trying to find full-time work. And, as you pointed out earlier, I left you with quite a few wedding bills I didn't think about." He drained the last of his coffee, glad she'd thought to order it.

"Still. I said I'd pay."

"Consider it paid. No more discussion." Nathan accepted back his card and the receipts, leaving a large tip before scribbling his name at the bottom. "Are you ready?"

She glared at him for another minute, then nodded her acquiescence.

Back down the elevator—or as he liked to refer to it, the torture chamber. Why anyone would think it was a good idea to create something so tall out of glass, he had no idea. He tried to stare more up than out or down, hoping it would ease the terror creeping up through his feet and inching toward his brain.

Bree's fingers wove through his and squeezed. Much as he didn't want to admit it, the simple touch kept the nervousness at bay a tiny bit. He tugged her a bit closer. Surely they were close to the ground by now, right?

Nope, out the window was still mostly sky. And the heavens were much brighter than he was accustomed to after eight in the evening. It took him a few minutes to realize it was because they were closer to the opposite end of the time zone from where he lived. That made sunset almost an hour later here than in Nashville.

"Still pretty warm out here, huh?" Bree stepped off the elevator as if her legs weren't turned to jelly. Maybe she was the stronger of the two of them.

"Mind if we call my mom in the parking lot? She seemed to want to talk as soon as possible." He held up his phone.

"Of course I don't mind." Bree followed him to the car and started the ignition while he walked around to the driver's seat. At least they'd have a bit of air conditioning while he figured out what had his mama in such a tizzy.

Mom picked up on the first ring. "Nathan."

"Hey, Mom. What's up?" He tried to act like his life was its normal boring self, hoping she wouldn't hear through the act.

"What's up? What do you mean by asking such an inane question? Are you or are you not with the girl who's supposed to be my daughter-in-love right now?"

His eyes sought out Bree's and must have looked rather panicked because she lifted her brows in question.

"Nathan Everette Hart!"

He held the phone away from his ear and cringed. Only one way could she have found out whom he was with. His brother moved another step down on his list of favorite people.

Bree grabbed his device and punched the speaker button before he could press it back to his ear. "Hey, Mama Hart."

"Bree!" His mom never sounded that excited to talk to him.

"What's wrong?" Bree glanced his way, and he realized how close she'd leaned to be able to share the phone.

"What do you think's wrong?" Not that his mother let them get a word in to answer. "Josh called earlier and let me in on some knowledge about the two of you being together in Dallas the last few days. And I just had to check and see for myself. What's going on?"

"It's a long story." Nathan let his head fall back against the headrest. "Your informant decided to play matchmaker and coerce us both into taking the honeymoon trip I'd booked since I couldn't get my money back. He didn't take into consideration … well, a lot of things."

"Like hurricanes." Bree's laugh filled the car. "When we ran into each other at the airport on Saturday, we figured out what Josh and Skye and Katie were up to, but by then, all the flights were canceled for the day due to the storms coming through. I decided to just play tourist for a few days here, and … well … so did Nathan."

Her big blue eyes looked his way as if to ensure she hadn't said something she wasn't supposed to.

He lifted as much of his lips as he could, hoping it looked close enough to a smile to ease her mind.

"You stayed there … together?" His mama's voice had all sorts of implications Nathan wasn't about to own up to.

"Separate hotel rooms." She ought to know him better than that.

"Of course." He could almost picture her brushing her hair back, acting like she hadn't just implied he'd been living in sin all week.

"Is that all you needed, Mama?"

"Well, actually, when Josh said you were heading back by car, I was thinking about how close you'll come to my house on your way. You know the interstate runs right through Texarkana when you're going from Dallas to Tennessee—"

"And you think we should stop and see you." He finished for her.

"Well, I mean, only if you have time, of course." Her words said it was no big deal, but her voice held a hint of longing.

"I don't know if Bree would want to have this rental car for an extra day. I mean, they're not as cheap as you might think, you know."

It wasn't that he didn't love his mother and wouldn't go

see her at any other time. It was more the awkwardness of the whole situation.

"I don't mind. I'd love to see Mama Hart again."

"When are y'all headed back?" If his mom wasn't bouncing in her seat right now, he'd eat his belt.

"Tomorrow, actually."

"Oh, good. Want to be here by lunch? I can fix your favorites. And we can grill out for supper." Meaning Nathan could stand in the heat and man the grill. "I'll change the sheets in Josh's room for Bree, and he can bunk with you for the night, Nathan."

"I'd hate to kick Josh out of his bed." Bree twisted a curl around her finger, distracting Nathan from any protests he might have otherwise made.

"Oh, don't worry about Josh. I'm sure he'd be glad to let you have that bed for the night. It'll be just like old times."

"Serves Josh right anyway. He's the one who got us into this whole mess." Nathan muttered the words, figuring they'd probably still carry through the phone. After all, his mama had ears sharper than a razor.

Bree smirked in response. "We'll see you tomorrow, then, Mama Hart. I'll let you know if we end up running late or anything."

"Thank you, darling." His mama paused, and a sniffle came through the speaker. "Oh, I'm so glad you two are back together."

Before either could correct her or offer any protests, she'd said her goodbyes and hung up. Tension filled up the small space of the vehicle in the remaining silence. They still sat close, the now-blank phone between them. Bree's expression flitted from humor to something else he couldn't quite make out in the deepening shadows around them.

"Guess we better get a good night's sleep." He buckled his

seatbelt. "Lots of correcting to do tomorrow."

Bree pinched her lips together. "Right."

The drive back to the hotel was quiet, as each of them seemed to be lost in their own thoughts. They parked and made their way into the hotel. On the second floor, quite a few people joined them in the elevator, pushing Bree into Nathan's side. He automatically wrapped an arm around her and pulled her closer.

At their floor, they wiggled through the mob and out into the silent hallway. His heart rate accelerated as they approached her door. The enchanted evening was at a close, and he wasn't sure how to end it gracefully.

"This is me." Bree tugged him to a stop and pulled her keycard out.

He hadn't even realized he'd still had her tucked into his side until she stepped away. Despite how hot he'd been all day, he missed the warmth of her under his arm. She pushed her door open and turned to give him one last smile.

Before she could slip inside, he caught her hand and leaned over, pressing his lips to hers. At first, she stiffened, and it dawned on him he had no right to this anymore—that he'd given it up a month before. But then she softened underneath his caress, and he stepped just a bit closer, reveling in the sense of rightness at having her here, with him.

They pulled apart slowly, her eyes a bit hazy. Much the same as his felt. He ran a finger down her cheek and tweaked one of the curls that had been distracting him all evening. She stepped back into her room, looking a bit lost.

"See you in the morning?" He whispered.

She nodded.

He moved back so she could close the door.

Had he just made the biggest mistake of his life? Or was he finally fixing it?

18

The light of day had things looking much different than the sunset glow the evening before. Nathan draped an arm across his eyes and groaned. Had last night seriously happened?

Maybe he could blame it on his migraine and all the painkillers he'd taken.

No.

Bree would never believe that. She'd seen him after a migraine too many times and knew better. Besides, except for the whole being-way-too-high-in-the-air thing, he couldn't deny he'd enjoyed most of the previous evening. Even part of the afternoon, for that matter.

Not that any of it had been the plan.

A message lit up his phone.

Will you be here for lunch?

Mom.

He squinted at the tiny numbers near the top of his phone.

From Dallas to Texarkana was around two and a half hours, depending on traffic. It was just after seven. Lunch would be doable if they left by nine.

Sure.

As an afterthought, he texted Bree to make sure she'd be ready by then. He probably could've knocked on the door between the rooms and asked her in person but wasn't quite ready to face her yet. How did she view their relationship now?

Stupid question when he wasn't even sure himself.

Sounds good to me.

Bree's reply came quickly, and he could almost picture her perky smile.

He set the phone down and went to shower, but a knock had him pausing. It came again, and he could tell it was from the adjoining doors instead of the hallway. So much for waiting a bit longer. Letting out a deep breath, he pushed the lock aside and turned the knob.

And there she was, her hair unbrushed, PJs made of a T-shirt and shorts, and a smile that looked a bit unsure. "Hi. I wondered if you might want to go down and get breakfast in a bit."

He tore his eyes away from her legs that looked so much longer than usual in that get-up, and raised them back to her face. "Um."

"You okay? I know I didn't wake you. You texted me first, remember?" She reached up and smoothed out a hair on top of his head that must've been standing on end.

How was he supposed to reply after that? And what was the question again?

"Nathan?" Bree tilted her head.

"Right. Sorry. Um. Breakfast. Sure." He glanced over his shoulder at the clock. "Give me half an hour or so? I need a shower."

"Sure. That'll give me time to do something with this mess." She lifted one of her brown strands with a wrinkled nose.

"It's not that bad." His hand reached out as if it had a mind of its own and smoothed a section of her hair. "Rather cute, really."

"You too." One corner of her lips lifted.

He stared at her with what was probably the goofiest grin of his life on his face. What was wrong with him this morning? It wasn't like they hadn't kissed before—hundreds of times. But last night felt different.

"So, half an hour?" Her voice came out a little breathless.

"Right." He shook out of his stupor. "Meet you then."

The door shut with a bit more force than necessary, but he needed the barrier it provided. She was under his skin, just as much if not more than when he'd first fallen for her. And it wasn't at all what he meant to happen when he saw her in the airport five days before.

It couldn't be.

A shower. He needed a shower. And maybe some caffeine.

Because, knowing how his mom operated, nothing would be easier when he got to her house. If anything, she'd probably make it harder to resist getting back into as much trouble as he'd been in before. And how much worse would the fallout be this time?

The same reasons he had before for not getting married still existed. But for some reason, they seemed less substantive. Why was that?

"Ugh. Josh, what did you get me into?" He banged his head against the shower wall as the steamy water pounded his back.

And he still had two more days to spend with Bree before he could drop her in Memphis. How was that supposed to work?

With his luck, his mama would kick him out of the house and keep Bree instead. She'd been so excited when they first got engaged. Afterward, though she still talked to him and loved him just like always, he could tell she didn't understand and was hurt.

Things might get really ugly over the next twenty-four hours if he wasn't careful.

But he was out of time to think about it. The clock kept ticking, and Bree would be waiting for breakfast. He flipped off the water and got as ready as he could to face the day.

It was just Bree. The girl he'd known for over three years now. Why was he so nervous?

Because, one way or another, everything was about to change.

***

Bree wavered between hope and uncertainty.

Nathan was quiet at breakfast, answering only when she asked him a question. But she couldn't deny how nice it was earlier when he'd been struck speechless at the sight of her in pajamas. Not that she wanted him to want her only for her physical appearance, but she might as well use all the cards in her deck since she had them.

With her last few items in the bag, she zipped it shut. Now that they were headed back to reality—via a stop at his mom's house—fear niggled at the edges of her heart. Had all of this simply been a vacation romance, doomed to end once the trip did?

Katie had wondered the same thing about Camden, but they were working out. Granted, they lived less than fifteen minutes from each other, which helped. But Bree and Nathan lived almost four hours apart.

"Stop it, Breanna Grace Henley." She glared at herself in the mirror. "'No use crying 'til you're actually bit,' as your granny would say."

A knock at the door interrupted her self-pep-talk. Time to face the future and see what it held. Maybe, just maybe, things would work out okay.

Nathan took her rolling suitcase from her hand and wheeled his on the other side as they made their way down the elevators and across the lobby one last time. He stashed their luggage in the trunk of the little rental car and opened the passenger door for her. Despite all the craziness that happened here, Bree couldn't help but glance around with eyes suspiciously moist as they exited the parking garage.

Rain drummed a steady rhythm on the roof as Nathan worked his way through traffic and onto I-30, heading east.

"Funny how it was raining when we came and raining when we're leaving." Bree nodded toward the weather.

"Fitting, isn't it?"

"How so?" She turned more toward him, glad he was engaging in conversation finally.

"Considering how turbulent and unsettled everything has been with us this week?" He lifted a shoulder before switching lanes to get out from behind a semi. "Seems like it's mimicking our ... relationship."

"But—" She stopped as she realized what he meant.

She'd begun to think maybe they were headed towards sunnier skies in their love life, but apparently, he still deemed things unsettled. Gray, dull, depressing, and soggy. Definitely her outlook now that she knew. So much for seeing eye to eye.

What had she missed?

That kiss.

Closing her eyes, she savored the memory for a moment. It had been so perfect. Unexpected, considering everything they'd gone through earlier in the week, but still ... It gave her a sense of coming home, of being cherished and wanted and maybe getting things back to the way she'd thought they should be.

Now she had even less of an idea what would happen.

And how awkward would it be when they got to his mom's house?

A text beeped through on her phone. Katie.

> Hey, girl. Do I get to see you tonight?

So sorry. Forgot to let you know. Stopping in Texarkana for the night. Be home tomorrow.

Memphis—home? Was it really? Sure, she loved Katie and enjoyed rooming with her. But Katie was starting her own life. New job, new boyfriend, new city. And half the time, Bree didn't fit.

Nashville was supposed to be Bree's next stop in life. It's what she'd planned for almost a year—ever since Nathan got the job with the firm he was at now. When they'd picked out the apartment together over spring break, she'd spent hours daydreaming where everything would go and what it would look like.

But instead of sharing a double bed with her husband, she was still stuck in a twin. *How much longer, God? I thought I understood what you wanted from me. Where am I supposed to go from here?*

A psalm she memorized as a teenager—lovingly given to her by her mother while waiting to see if she'd made the cheerleading team—popped into her head. The last verse of chapter 27. "Wait for the Lord; be strong, and let your heart take courage; wait for the Lord!"

It hadn't been easy then, and it wouldn't be easy now either.

But what else could she do? If Nathan couldn't see what was literally sitting right next to him, she couldn't force him to look. No. Stooping to that level wouldn't lead to either of them being any happier.

Because when people married for the wrong reasons, more often than not, their marriages failed. It was one of the reasons they'd done premarital counseling with one of their Bible professors. That, and the discount they'd get on the marriage license fee.

"What went wrong?"

"What?" Nathan glanced at her with a frown.

Oops. She hadn't meant to ask that out loud. "Nothing."

He sent another curious glance her way before returning his gaze to the road. The rain let up, but the skies looked like it could start again any minute. She knew the feeling. Her eyes echoed the moisture.

Maybe if she changed the subject, they could at least break the silence and she wouldn't have to think. "Wonder if the rain will follow us there. Your mom said something about you grilling."

"Knowing her, she'll just park me under the gazebo on the back porch and have me do it anyway. It'd take a hurricane to stop her once she's got her mind made up."

"Guess we're a few days too late, then, huh?" Bree chuckled. "The hurricane was last Saturday."

"Huh." The sound came out somewhere between a laugh and a sigh. "Guess that's right."

And the conversation lagged again. Could she do this all the way to the other side of Texarkana? They'd only been in the car forty minutes. Wasn't it more than two hours to get there?

"Want some music?" Nathan leaned forward and messed with the knobs.

"Sure. Need me to handle that while you steer?"

"Okay, but I get veto rights if you pick something I don't like." The edge of his lip tilted up in that way she loved so much.

It took her back to when they first started hanging out and he'd almost kicked her out of the car one night when she tried to change out his music list for hers. After that, he made sure she understood the driver was in charge, even if the navigator had to work the controls for him. Dating had loosened him up only a little.

But she remembered what he liked. And after three or four staticky stations, she landed on one that should keep them both happy. At least it would kill the infernal silence. Not to mention the compulsion to find something to talk about, which only led to painful conversations.

Just under two hours to his mom's house, if she did her math right at the next road sign. Maybe God wanted her to use this time to pray. It would be a better use of resources than attempting to get any pleasantness from the driver.

If only she could quit wondering what Mama Hart would assume when they walked in together.

19

"Oh, my girl!" Mama Hart wrapped Bree in a hug possibly larger than one her own mother would give. Despite Bree's petite size, Mama Hart was a few inches shorter, her brown hair mostly silvered now, and pulled back in a French braid. She wasn't fat by any means but was thick enough to be comfortable.

"Mom, give her room to breathe." Josh's chuckle came from the other side of the kitchen.

"She can breathe." But she stepped back and placed a hand on either side of Bree's face. "How are you, darling?"

So many answers came to mind. But how could Bree confess to Nathan's mom she was afraid he would break her heart again? Or that she was a swirl of just about every emotion known to man, plus a few experienced only by women?

"You haven't been eating enough. I can see it. Your cheeks are thinner." Her silvery eyes, so much like Nathan's, studied Bree's until she feared Mama Hart would see straight through to the memories of the last few days.

"I'm okay." Bree decided her answer was more social convention than little white lie.

"Good to see you, too, Mama." Nathan nudged them both out of the doorway and carried in their two suitcases. "And yes, I'd love some lunch. Maybe something warm to kill off the chill of this lovely reception."

His mom raised an eyebrow and tucked one hand into a hip. "You know I'm always glad to see you. But Bree. I never thought I'd get to see her again. So forgive me if I try to snatch up every second."

Nathan pinched his lips together and moved their luggage down the hallway.

The three or four times Bree had visited this house, nothing but love, warmth, and kindness made up the atmosphere. Just now, Mama Hart added a chilly note. Was she mad at Nathan for calling off their wedding?

"Don't be too hard on him." Bree touched the arm of the woman she'd expected to have as a mother-in-law, almost surprised at the words that came out of her mouth.

"Sometimes he needs someone to be hard enough to wake him up so he can see reality again."

"And sometimes he needs to be reminded that he's loved no matter what." Bree swallowed the tears threatening. "Excuse me a minute. I'm going to go borrow your restroom."

She didn't have to look to know Josh and Mama Hart were exchanging confused glances behind her. Locked inside the pristine powder room, she leaned against the door and allowed a few tears to escape. Maybe if she eased some of the pressure behind the dam of emotion, a flood wouldn't occur when she reemerged.

Where had those words come from? It had to be God. She'd prayed for almost two hours straight as the music played and Nathan hadn't said a word. And while she hadn't gotten a complete sense of peace, she had gotten more confidence in her ability to handle whatever came next.

But most of all, as she'd prayed, her words turned from asking God for what she wanted to asking Him to heal whatever was wrong in Nathan. Because until that was fixed, their relationship didn't need to go anywhere else. And once she accepted that, it was easier to simply bring the man she loved before the God who loved them both. If anyone cared about and could fix this mess, it was Him.

A few minutes later, emotions mostly back under control, she searched out the family in the kitchen. Wonderful aromas came from a large pot on the stove, and she inhaled deeply. The two boys and their mom all turned from what seemed to be a rather heated discussion as she joined them at the island.

"Ready for lunch?" Mama Hart bustled around as if nothing else had taken place before Bree came in.

"It smells wonderful."

"Just sloppy joes. Nothing fancy. But it used to be one of Nathan's favorites." She pressed a plate into Bree's hand and waved her toward the buns and meat.

"One of mine too."

"Just wait until tonight. With Nathan here, we can finally grill those pork tenderloins I've had in the freezer. And I'll whip up some potato salad and green beans fresh from the garden."

"My mouth's already watering thinking about it." Bree grinned and took a big bite of the best sloppy joe she'd ever had.

"How am I supposed to grill when it's pouring down rain?" Nathan pointed out the window.

His mom waved off the question like a pesky gnat. "I had Josh move the grill under the gazebo."

Bree almost choked as she laughed at the very thing

Nathan said would happen. He shot her a dirty look, but she couldn't quell the giggles. Surely even he could see the humor in it.

Maybe not.

"I want to hear all about your time in Dallas." Mama Hart settled on a stool across from Bree. "What all did you do? It's been a long time since I visited there."

"We checked out the Farmer's Market on Sunday afternoon." Bree smiled. "It was the most amazing one I've ever been to. The food was delicious, and there were all sorts of hand-made crafts and booths full of fun things."

"My son went to a farmer's market willingly?"

"He did." Bree pulled up a few photos she'd taken of the two of them, Nathan glaring at the camera in each one. "And though he doesn't look happy here, he enjoyed it too."

"He'd be so handsome if he'd only smile more."

"Monday, we visited the museum where Kennedy was shot. And the Arboretum." Bree scrolled through the pictures of the flowers and fountains. A few included the two of them again; some even had Nathan without a scowl.

"Going to tell her how you got food poisoning?" Nathan added the one part Bree had hoped to avoid.

"Only if you mention your migraine Tuesday afternoon." Two could play at that game.

He narrowed his eyes at her.

His mom darted her attention between the two of them, a look of surprise on her face. "Oh my. Sounds like a rough time. But you're okay?"

"Fine. Just some bad Chinese food. It really only bothered me a few hours." Bree used a potato chip to scoop up some filling that had dropped on her plate.

"A whole evening."

Bree ignored him. "The next morning, we went on a carriage ride."

There went that glare again. Obviously, Nathan hadn't meant for that part to be included either.

"Then to a park where there were games to rent and food trucks. And I explored Deep Ellum for a while—lots of murals to look at." Those pictures were a bit more awkward. For some reason, she'd forgotten about the one where they filled in the equation for love. His mom's hand stopped her before she could scroll past it.

"Oh."

Now what? What should she say about their dinner the night before? Was it too much in line with what his mother hoped? Would Nathan hate her if she mentioned it?

"You forgot that crazy eyeball." Nathan didn't meet her gaze.

"Right." She pulled up the photo. "I couldn't resist stopping when we spotted it. I had to take a picture to send to Skye. It's right up her alley."

"You two are so cute." His mom sighed. "And you look so happy in these last few pictures. Almost exactly like when you had your engagement photos taken last fall."

Bree's heart skipped. Was it true? She hadn't even looked that closely at the pictures they'd taken on the trip. Definitely hadn't compared the two. But now that it had been pointed out, she couldn't deny the truth.

Would Nathan agree? Would it change anything?

"You want to tell me what's going on?"

Nathan turned from the kitchen window where he'd been staring at Bree talking with Josh out on the back porch. The rain had let up right after he'd finished grilling, of course. His Mom leaned against the island, the look on her face telling him he wasn't getting out of this easily.

"Is something going on?" He tried to play nonchalant. "I mean besides Josh trying to set me up with my ex-fiancée."

"I've already had a talk with Josh, bless his heart." His mom tapped the edge of the counter. "He had good intentions but didn't quite think them all through. God gave that boy the romantic inclinations of his grandmother with none of the good sense to offset them."

He'd missed his mother's unique way of putting things.

"So, now we get to discuss you. And why exactly you called things off with that girl when you so obviously love her."

"Love has nothing to do with anything." He turned around, pulled some of the clean dishes from the drainer, and started putting them away.

"And just how do you go about figuring that?" Mom stilled his hands by taking them into hers. "I need some answers, and I think Bree does too."

"I gave you answers when it first happened." He couldn't meet her eyes.

"No. You gave excuses. And, quite honestly, they fell rather flat."

His head jerked her way as the desire to argue rose. So much for not looking up.

"No, sir." She shook a finger in his face. "I've known you all twenty-three years of your life, and you might have initially been upset about those boys hanging out on their girls' trip, but you were over it by the time you used it as an excuse to break things off with her. Now tell me what really happened."

His mouth opened and closed again as he debated trying to get away with telling her anything else that wasn't the whole truth. The longer he hesitated, though, the fiercer she became. No. Only the truth would do.

"Dad called."

Mom took a step back.

Even mentioning the man to her sat like a rock in his gut. "Right around the time she was gone. He'd gotten the invitation to the wedding. Gave some excuse about not being able to make it."

"Selfish ..." Her mutterings held touches of words she'd never let him get away with saying, but he didn't dare point that out.

"Anyway." He tugged at a longer piece of hair on top of his head. "Then he went on about how I was just wasting my time going through all the 'hoopla,' I believe is what he called it. Said I could get everything I wanted without actually getting married, and then I wouldn't leave behind such a mess when it didn't work out."

"He. Did. Not."

"He did." Nathan glanced out the window again. Bree laughed at something his brother said and Nathan couldn't help but be jealous of their easy camaraderie. Nothing had been easy between Bree and Nathan in months.

"And you let him ruin your marriage?" Tears of anger welled in her eyes. "Wasn't it enough he ruined his own? He shouldn't have that power!"

He caught her fist before it hit the counter, not wanting her to hurt herself. "Stop, Mama. It's okay. It wasn't really what he said that made me call things off. It was the realization that I might end up just like him. And I didn't want Bree to have to deal with everything you've gone through just because she married someone who turned out to be as big a jerk as his father."

Mom stepped back and slashed her hand through the air. "No!"

Honestly, he was a little scared. Her fury had turned a bit vicious.

"You listen to me." She took his chin in her hand and squeezed.

He had to lean over a few inches so it didn't hurt.

"You are not your father."

"But—"

"No. You are *not* him. And I raised you better than that. So, you won't turn into him either."

She released him and grabbed some hot pads. That was it? That was supposed to fix everything? But it didn't.

"I might not be him, but that doesn't mean I know how to be better than he was, either. He was my example. The only dad I've ever known. How am I supposed to be a good husband or father when I was never shown how?" His arms flopped at his sides.

"He wasn't your only example." Mom scoffed at him even while pulling a peach crisp from the oven.

"I don't see any other husbands in your life for me to emulate." Nathan motioned around them.

"Maybe not here, but at church, yes. You saw how all those husbands treated their wives. You had your grandfathers until you were in college. You've seen Bree's dad. You've got other friends getting married and can hang out with them." His mom shook her head and squeezed his arm. "You're not alone."

He inched over to a stool and eased up onto it. Was she right? But there were still so many ways things could go wrong. It was too big a risk.

"Nathan, look at me."

It took him a minute to do what she demanded.

"You also have your heavenly Father. And He gave you tons

of advice in the Bible. I know you know that." She held up a finger as she started mentioning scriptures. "Leave your parents and cling to your spouse. Be fruitful and give your mama some grandbabies to love."

"That's not what it says."

"Close enough."

And the look on her face said he better not argue with her interpretation.

"Be faithful to each other. Don't even look at another person to lust after them. Love each other as Christ loved the church."

"What if I can't love her like that?" So much anguish welled up in him at the thought that the query came out no louder than a whisper.

"Silly boy. You already do." His mama somehow managed to wrap him up in her arms like she used to when he was younger, despite how much taller he was now. "I heard those stories about Dallas. Even got a few more out of Bree this afternoon.

"When you almost got arrested for following her in the airport because you wanted to make sure she was safe. When you conquered your fears and took a rideshare to find her because you didn't trust the area she had ventured off to. You put her above yourself in those cases. Put yourself in danger to keep her safe. If that isn't love, I don't know what is."

Could it be true?

He'd already accepted the idea of leaving her in Memphis the next day was slaughtering his heart. Maybe the answer was not leaving her. But first, before they could go any further, she needed the truth too.

"I don't know how I can admit to her ..." He glanced toward the back porch.

"Here." His mama dished up a portion of the sweet dessert

and topped it off with vanilla ice cream. "Take this to sweeten things up."

"Food doesn't always fix things."

"No. But it makes the truth go down a little easier." She patted his hand around the bowl. "And don't expect her to be able to accept it right away. It's taken you this long to get through it. Give her time and grace too."

Time and grace.

God, help me here? I can't do this on my strength alone. Give me the words. Let Mama be right.

20

Carrying two bowls of hot and cold desserts had his hands complaining quickly. He pushed through the screen door and headed for the swing.

"Ooh, is that for me?" Josh jumped up and reached for one, but Nathan spun around and deflected the steal.

"Nope. You're a big boy. Go get your own." He nodded back toward the kitchen. "Mom's dishing it up now."

"I'm glad I'm not considered a big boy—it's nice to have someone else bring you dessert." Bree accepted one of the dishes and sent a smile his way.

"Definitely not a boy, big or otherwise."

Since being around his family, some of the awkwardness that hitchhiked with them from Dallas that morning had dissipated. She still didn't act completely sure around him, though. Not like before ...

And it was his fault. Because he let his father's ugly words and history get into his head and convince him he wasn't any better. But how to explain that to Bree without widening the rift he'd already formed between them?

"May I?" He nodded toward the spot his brother had vacated.

"Of course." She tucked her feet under her and then took a big bite of the peach crisp. "Mm. Your mom is one of the best cooks I know. Think she'd let me come visit every summer just so I can learn from her?"

"Pretty sure she'd welcome you with open arms." He glanced through the kitchen window and caught a glimpse of his mom waving at him, as if sending positive vibes. "I think she's about to disown me and claim you as hers instead."

"Surely not." Bree paused with the spoon halfway to her mouth. "You're her first baby. She'd never get rid of you."

"I don't know." He used the excuse of chewing his own bite to buy a few extra moments. "When we got engaged, she told me if anything were to happen between us, she'd keep you instead of me."

Bree stilled, as if unsure how serious he was.

"She was mostly teasing." He winked.

"Right." And with that, she unfroze and started eating again. "I guess I'm in, then, huh?"

"Guess so."

"Good to know."

For a few minutes, the only sounds around them were the crickets and frogs singing in the yard and the scrape of their spoons against their bowls. He was at a loss as to how to broach the subject. How could he explain why he called off a wedding when it had been more than a month since it happened?

"You're thinking awfully hard over there." Bree's voice was soft as she set her bowl on the small table in front of them, where a citronella candle flickered.

"Trying to figure out how to say this." He added his bowl to hers and then leaned forward, his elbows on his knees.

"Are you about to tell me that once you drop me off tomorrow, that's it?" Her whisper was so soft, he barely caught it all.

"No." Spinning around to face her, he grabbed her hands. "No."

She nodded, but her lips trembled, and he could've punched himself for causing her any more worry or pain. Though what he needed to say might heap on a few more piles before all was said and done. Resituating to where their knees touched and their fingers intertwined, he took a deep breath. No more procrastinating.

"I owe you an explanation."

Her hands jerked back, but he held tight, needing to feel her close for a few minutes more.

"You kept asking me why I wanted to call things off."

"And you said it was because you couldn't trust me."

One nod. "The more accurate way to say it was that I didn't trust me."

A furrow burrowed through her forehead as her brows dipped down. "What do you mean?"

"You know my dad cut out when I was around seven years old. He's never been a big part of my life. Hardly even recognizes birthdays or anything."

"Right."

"Well, Mom thought we should go ahead and add him to the list of wedding invitees." Nathan couldn't look at her, couldn't face her expressions as he did this. "He called me right about the time y'all left for your last girls' trip. Said he got his invitation."

Was she breathing? He couldn't hear anything over the pounding of his heartbeat in his ears.

"He said he wasn't going to bother coming and that I was wasting my time getting married. That marriage wasn't worth the hassle. Several other things like that. Anyway, he told me it was much easier to just not get married because then I wouldn't leave behind a big mess when things didn't work out."

Bree squeezed his hands until he looked up. "I don't understand."

"Don't understand what?" The emotion clogging his throat made it hard to talk.

"Why that would make you change your mind. If it were me, I'd want to prove him wrong. Show him marriage and family are more than just messes to leave behind when you decide life would be easier without them."

An airy laugh escaped him. "Of course you would. Because you're stronger than I am."

"You're not—"

He lifted their fingers and pressed them to her lips to keep her from defending him. Not until she knew everything. He'd say the rest and then see how she felt afterward.

"I'm not like you. I'm a numbers guy. I look at realities and outcomes and estimate future outcomes from those figures. So, when he started talking like that, it reminded me how I didn't have a real dad in my life growing up—hadn't had a father I could look up to and see how a husband was supposed to behave or act."

She squeaked, but he continued talking, not letting her protest.

"I didn't want you to end up going through any of what my mom has gone through since her husband left her. No one deserves that, but especially not the woman I love. And I didn't trust myself enough to be sure I wouldn't end up just like the man who came before me."

"But you're not like him." She finally got her words in between his.

"But he is part of the equation I come from. Half him and

half Mom. That means there is at least some of him and his tendencies inside me too."

Bree shook her head, mouth open.

"I'm not saying it was the best decision, but it's where it came from. I just didn't want to admit all of it back then. Couldn't tell you how ashamed I was of my dad and how afraid I was that he'd had more influence in my life than he should.

"So, when you started talking about those guys who tagged along with you, I guess I shifted my anger to them and used them as an excuse. Especially when I showed up to surprise you in Germantown that Saturday and saw you hugging Camden."

Bree's mind spun in circles, gaining no traction. He called off their wedding because he was afraid? He'd let her believe a lie for the last month, blaming Camden, blaming her, when really it was his own timid heart that couldn't face a future with her.

She pulled her fingers free and scratched them through her hair. "I explained over and over and over again about Camden."

"I know." His voice was quiet, calm. Too calm.

"And when we ran into each other at DFW, you challenged me to prove to you that I didn't even look at the other guys on the road trip."

"Which you did and didn't." His lips twitched as if fighting a laugh.

Well, she wasn't ready for laughing yet. She crossed her arms over her chest and leaned back. "Oh really? And how is that, oh mighty one? What makes you such a great judge?"

"Well, you proved to me you couldn't have had any interest

in the other guys because you definitely had some interest in the idiot who tagged along on this road trip with you."

A squeak erupted from her chest. She hated it when she did that.

"You know it's true."

"True or not, that doesn't make any of this better. Besides, that idiot who tagged along with me seemed to have some mutual interest too."

He rubbed the back of his neck and ducked his head. "Ye-ah."

Somewhere, the circles in her head gained a bit of traction. "Do you mean to tell me that we could have been married already? If you'd talked to me or someone about any of this and worked it out, we could've gone through with the wedding."

His mouth opened, but nothing came out.

She jumped from the swing and started pacing the small porch.

All that work she had to do to cancel everything, to try and get some of the money back, to return wedding gifts. The dress hanging in her closet, mocking her for the last month, could've been worn in all its glory less than a week ago. She could've been sharing a room with him instead of staring at a door separating them.

"We could've been married."

"I thought I was doing what was best for you."

"You didn't even ask if I agreed with that assessment of things. I didn't even know what happened. I've been miserable for over a month now, trying to figure out how *I* messed up my happily ever after. And then I find out *I* didn't do anything wrong."

"Bree." He stood and reached out for her, but she yanked back.

"Don't Bree me, mister." She wagged a finger in his direction. "Sure. I know your dad was a jerk. And I hate he did that to you. But, as I said earlier, you're not him. And he's not the only husband you had as an example, you know."

"Mom pointed that out a little while ago."

Bree pressed her palms to her lips to try and hold in a scream of frustration. "All those premarital counseling sessions and none of this came up. Not a word. Nothing about how you were afraid you might turn out like your dad. Or ruin our marriage somehow."

"I know." He stepped back and tugged at the long hairs on top of his head. "I'm sorry."

"I'm sorry too. But I can't ... I can't handle this right now. I don't even know what to think, what to feel. Did you even still want to marry me?" She slashed a hand through the air. "No. Don't answer that."

He waited a moment as if expecting her to change her mind. Well, she wasn't going to. Couldn't take anymore right now.

"I'm sorry I keep hurting you. I honestly did everything to try and not hurt you." He gathered up their dirty dishes. "I'll leave you alone now. Goodnight, Bree."

The unsaid *I love you* echoed through the space despite it not being issued. Did he love her? At one point in time, his love for her had been the most certain thing in her life, after God. Now, she had to wonder. Because his fear had been stronger.

"And perfect love casts out fear," she whispered to the backyard before collapsing on the swing.

For so long, she'd wanted to know the real reason he'd called things off. Thought if she knew why, then she could somehow fix it. But how was a girl supposed to fix this?

Part of her wanted to call his dad and tell him a thing or two, but she knew that would only make matters worse. Movement at the kitchen window drew her attention, and she caught Mama Hart looking out at her, a worried expression on her face. But this wasn't something she could fix, either. Not even with another helping of that delicious peach crisp.

"Stubborn, stubborn man!"

Why hadn't he talked to her earlier? Or anyone. Because his mom had evidently helped him see some reason, or he might not've ever told Bree the truth either.

As much as she'd hated the idea of him dropping her off the next day and never seeing her again, she hated this more. It was like she'd seen a glimpse of paradise but didn't have a boat to cross over to it. Besides, she'd cut him off before he could answer her question about wanting to marry her. That had been foolish, too, because she wanted to know.

"God, I don't know what to do." Her head dropped to her knees, and she wrapped her arms around her shins. "I thought everything was crazy and confused at the beginning of this trip, but it was nothing compared to this."

"Bree." Mama Hart stuck her head out the door. "I hate to interrupt, but they're saying more rain's on the way soon."

Slowly she unfolded and followed the woman she'd hoped would be her mother-in-law into the house. She could've been! And that hurt too. Because Mama Hart made her feel like family anyway.

"Thanks for the dessert." Bree leaned into a hug from the older woman. "It was great."

"Don't give up on him yet, dear one." Mama Hart didn't let go right away. "He's got some more soul searching to do, too, but if you both forgive, I think you'll come out of this stronger than before."

"I don't know how to move on from this." Bree's eyes started leaking again. When would this tear-fest stop already?

"With God's help. And by actually talking to each other." Mama Hart patted her cheek. "He made a big step by admitting as much as he did tonight. Now don't let him stop talking about things."

"I'm going back to ... well, Josh's room." Bree offered a semi-smile.

"Get some rest. And pray."

Bree paused at the doorway of Nathan's room. He glanced up, his eyes rather haunted. But she didn't know how to chase away the ghosts.

As she stepped into Josh's room and shut the door, the heavens opened outside and pounded on the roof. What had Nathan said earlier that morning? Turbulent and gloomy, indeed. And no sunshine in sight.

21

The thunderstorm against the metal roof echoed through the otherwise quiet house. The others had all turned in hours before, so far as she could tell, but Bree lay in bed tossing and turning, unsure which direction was up. How was a girl supposed to sleep when regrets and might-have-beens ran through her head as if training for a marathon?

She pulled her phone out and scrolled through the pictures she'd taken over the course of their trip. At first, most of them had been selfies, or with Nathan and her standing awkwardly beside each other as though unsure how close was too close. But those last few days? All those photos had happy faces. Beaming, really.

Like their engagement photos. Was Mama Hart right? She quickly scrolled down to the snapshot she'd shown the security officer at the airport. Had that been only a few days ago? But studying it, she could see definite similarities in expressions between the pictures where they knew they were in love and the ones from yesterday.

No telling what a picture of the two of them would look

like after tonight, though. She set the phone down once more and squeezed her eyes shut. Despite all the prayers she'd sent up, the only answer she'd gotten so far was silence.

A rapid rap at the door had her sitting up in the dark. "Who is it?"

"It's Nathan. Can I talk to you for a minute?"

"No" hovered on her tongue, set to cannonball through the air. But she reined it in. Not like she was sleeping anyway.

"I guess."

The door cracked, and then Nathan poked his head through, a nightlight in the hallway showing only his outline. But she would've recognized him anyway. She scooted back against the headboard as he made his way across the dark room, the door left open just a hair.

At the edge of the bed, he hesitated, seeming uncertain where to perch. A few nights before, he'd sat on the big hotel mattress with her with fewer qualms. How had they gone from that to this once again?

She patted the edge near her feet. "Might as well sit down. I assume you didn't just come in to say 'Hi' at"—a glance at the clock had her frowning—"twelve-thirty."

His weight on the old mattress caused her to slide towards him.

"Josh's bed hasn't been replaced in a while, huh?"

"No." Nathan ruffled his hair and sighed. "I just ... I didn't ..."

Bree rested her chin on her knees. What could he need? Was there anything left unsaid earlier worth staying up this late for?

"I couldn't sleep. Everything was so unsettled earlier, and I hated the thought of us trying to go to sleep with that hanging over us."

Very little light penetrated the blackout curtains covering the windows. Her eyes had adjusted to things just enough to make out the way he sat but not discern an expression. Lightning flashed outside bright enough to show the sorrow in his eyes.

Did hers look the same?

"I'm not sure there's anything we can say tonight to make it better." She kept her voice soft despite the loud rumble of thunder nearby.

He slumped.

This was so hard. Much as she hurt, she didn't mean to inflict pain on him. The phrase *Misery loves company* never had made sense to her. But could this be fixed?

Another rumble reminded them of the storm's presence. And took her back to memories of another occasion. When she and Nathan hadn't been estranged.

"Remember that time—" They both started at the same moment.

A giggle escaped her, and the effervescence of it lifted her spirits more than almost anything could have.

"You go ahead." He covered her hand with his, and she found she didn't want to move it.

"Remember that night when we were here a few years ago and a storm came through?"

Another flash lit up the grin on his lips. They'd been thinking of the same memory. He nodded. "We decided to watch a movie, but the power went out."

"You rounded up all your mom's candles and lit them around the living room. It was late at night—Mama Hart and Josh had gone to bed."

"And we snuggled on the couch, dreaming about what things would be like when we didn't have to say goodnight and go to separate rooms." His fingers twined through hers.

A tear wound its way down her cheek. "That could've been us this week."

"I know."

A clap of thunder, louder than the rest thus far, shook the house, and Bree jumped. She pressed a hand to her chest and breathed through her nose. He shifted and scooted closer, his back leaning against the headboard next to hers, shoulder to shoulder.

"Sounds like the storm's right on top of us now. Probably won't last much longer."

She nodded. "It just caught me off guard."

They were quiet a few minutes, and she almost wondered if he'd decided the conversation was over. Then he wiggled again, and his voice sounded near her ear. "Do you remember what you asked earlier and then didn't let me answer?"

How could she forget? She swallowed. Surely he wouldn't come in here, reminding her of sweeter times, and then break her heart—right?

"Yes."

"All those dreams we wove together, the talks about what we wanted our future to look like, the touches you already added to the apartment ... they're still here." He pressed her hand to his chest. "No matter what happens between the two of us, you, Bree, are always going to be here.

"I know this doesn't make things right. Or even offer a good solution. But I couldn't let you end the day without knowing." His head bonked against the wooden bed frame and a shudder rocked his torso. "I tried to convince myself that eventually it wouldn't hurt so much and that I was making the best choice." He shook his head. "But you're the only choice that's best for me."

The tears flowed freely now, and nothing would hold them back. And even if she'd known what to say, she probably couldn't inch the words past the clog in her throat. He pressed a kiss to her hands and then set them gently on the bed.

"Good night, Bree." Another kiss to her forehead, and then he was gone, as quietly as he'd come in.

God, what do I do? I can't just ignore everything that's happened. But I can't just let him go, either. I still love him so much.

Originally, the plan had been to leave after lunchtime since their drive would take only about four hours to return Bree to Memphis. But she was restless from the moment she got up, staring out a window, then moving to a stool in the kitchen, then perching on the edge of the sofa, then something else. And while all that time locked in a car probably wouldn't help her antsiness, maybe it would at least give her a purpose.

"I think we might need to pull out earlier than we'd discussed." Nathan murmured the words to his mama, and she nodded, her eyes following Bree as she paced the length of the dining room.

"You might be right." She crooked a finger at him and then led him down the hallway to her bedroom. "Did you two get anything settled last night? I heard you prowling about in the small hours of the morning."

"We didn't do anything wrong."

"I didn't say you did." She winked. "Besides, I know you weren't in there that long."

"I don't know that anything was settled from it anyway." He shifted. "I think she's more upset that we could've been married right now and aren't because I let my insecurities and worries get in the way."

"Perfect love casts out fear." The scripture came easily from his mom's mouth. She'd been through so much and yet still held to her faith and the belief that marriage was a good thing. How did she do it?

"Why did Dad get to me when he hasn't been able to break you?" Nathan leaned against the dresser. "You've had the harder end of the stick."

"You haven't seen me at my darkest moments." She sat on the edge of her bed. "I didn't want you and your brother to witness that. Maybe that was wrong, but I also knew I needed to be strong for you boys. Because you were growing up without a father figure, with no example of what a family should look like according to God's plan."

She smoothed her hand over the quilt. "That's one of the reasons I made sure you were both heavily involved at church. It surrounded you with godly men. And I rejoiced when you both decided to attend Freed-Hardeman University. Because I knew it would protect you from at least a few of the sins you might be tempted by at a state school."

"You've given up a lot for us." He frowned, already starting to think of ways he could help her put back some to be able to retire in the future.

"No more than any parent should." She brushed his words aside like the vapor they were. "But I also feel I've failed you. I didn't realize your father still had so much influence in your life. Otherwise I would've tried to combat it earlier. When you asked for the engagement ring that used to be my mama's, I hoped you would break the cycle of your father's family."

"I didn't tell you enough."

"No. But I should've asked more questions. I knew what you'd seen of my marriage and ought to have—"

"Mama, no. No more *oughts* or *should'ves* or *might'ves* either. That's getting us nowhere fast. We're here now. So, this is our starting point."

She pressed her lips together but gave a curt nod. "Okay, then. What's the plan?"

"I guess the plan is to drop Bree off at Katie's and then see what I can do long distance for a while. I broke her trust, and that's a hard-earned commodity. It won't be earned back quickly."

Holding up a finger, Mama moved to rummage through the bedside table. "I don't know but you might've already earned back a little bit simply by finally giving her the whole truth. How about I go ahead and give this back to you, just in case?"

He accepted the black velvet box warily. "Shouldn't we wait?"

"I don't want you to have to drive all the way out here again if you find you need it in a future closer than you expect. After all, you two do have hours left to drive together. No telling what might get worked out between here and the Mississippi River."

With a shake of his head, he slipped the jewelry into his pocket anyway. "Sometimes I wish I had your faith."

"Faith is grown, baby. It doesn't pop up overnight. You have to water it and give it sunshine." She patted his cheek. "Prayers and Bible reading and accepting that not everything works the way we think it should also helps."

Josh poked his head through the doorway. "Is Bree okay? She's acting a little like my dog did back when she first had puppies."

Nathan grimaced at that analogy. "She'll be okay. I think she's just ready to be home. Your bed isn't the most comfortable in the house, you know."

"Better than the floor of your room." Josh rolled his eyes.

"Maybe next time you won't be so ready to meddle where you shouldn't." Nathan bumped his brother's arm. "Or you could take an internship that lasts longer than a few weeks so you won't be home the same time I am."

Nathan searched the house until he found Bree on the back porch, exactly where she'd been the night before when he told her everything. He paused for a minute, soaking in her beauty—rather glad he hadn't been able to see her pajamas in the dark room the night before. Then he stepped out and eased onto the swing beside her.

"Whatcha think about heading out a little earlier than planned? We can just grab a bite to eat on the way."

She frowned. "Do you need to be back for something?"

"No. But you're acting like you need to be moving. I figured a car could get you there faster than your feet."

Her lips twitched. "I guess I'll go gather my things."

He nodded. "Sounds good."

It didn't take long to throw his few items back in the bag and have it at the door. As Bree came down the hallway with her luggage, Mama pulled her into a big hug. He reached to pick up her suitcase and overheard a few of the whispers his mom breathed in Bree's ear.

"Trust your heart. Work on this together. Don't bottle it all up inside like he did. That'll only cause another explosion. But he's a good boy, Bree. And you know y'all have my blessing if you decide to get back together." Mama leaned back and raised an eyebrow. "I'm even okay with an elopement if it gets you as my daughter faster."

Before Bree could turn around and see him close by, he made sure he took a few steps away. No need to embarrass her more. Or let her see his own embarrassment, for that matter.

"Ready?"

She glanced around the house once more, as if afraid she might not get to see it again. "Sure."

22

As Nathan maneuvered his way through traffic and out of Texarkana, the silence of the car promised nothing but a long trip ahead. Would it be as stilted and awkward as the drive from Dallas the day before? Or worse, now that she knew the whole truth?

How was he supposed to stand the next four hours in a car with Bree and not continue to try and win her back? Waiting had never been his strong suit. But she hadn't even turned her pretty face his way once since they left. That didn't bode well for his chances.

Speed limit sign.

Mile marker.

Semi-truck number fifty-three.

To keep from going mad, he listed each item silently in his head. On a normal day, Bree would probably participate in such a stupid game, laughing at each mundane thing. But nothing was typical about their situation right now.

"Oh!" Bree sat up straight and leaned forward.

He glanced over at the side of the road where she stared but didn't notice anything unusual.

"Did you see that sign?" There was more excitement in her voice than he'd heard in a while.

"No. What did it say?"

"Did you know diamonds came from Arkansas?"

"The sign said that?"

"No, silly." Bree motioned behind them. "It said there's a state park nearby where you can find diamonds."

He huffed a laugh. "That's what they claim anyway. I don't know anyone who's ever found one."

"Have you been?"

"To Crater of Diamonds? Sure. It's a field trip for every school within driving distance." He beat out a drum rhythm on the steering wheel. "I think that one happened in fourth grade."

"That's so cool. What's it like?" She craned her neck to look out the window as if the park were right outside instead of another half an hour of driving.

"It's hot. A big, empty field where you sit in the sun and use cheap tools to sift through old pieces of volcanic rock in the hopes of finding something that hasn't already been uncovered by the millions of others who have done the same thing." He rolled his eyes. "Not that fun."

"No sense of adventure or hope, huh?" Bree leaned back and tapped her slender finger on her chin. "Let's go."

"What?"

"Let's go see if we can find something no one else has found yet." As much as her seat belt allowed, she gave a little bounce.

"Bree, seriously. It's like the hottest place in Arkansas. And very few people find anything of value."

"Road trip rules are that if one person on the trip wants to do something, you have to at least look into it."

"There are rules to your road trips?"

"Of course there are."

"Of course there are." He muttered, knowing full well he was about to give in and do something he had no desire to do. Why should today be any different than the last five?

Hitting the turn signal, he took the exit for the state park. Despite the rain the night before, today was toasty. The sun already beat down on them, and not a cloud for miles to block any of the rays. He hummed a few bars of "I Would Do Anything for Love." It seemed appropriate.

"What if we find a diamond? That would definitely cover the cost of our trip, right?" Bree leaned forward, not that it made the car move any faster.

"Most of the diamonds found are tiny and imperfect. I don't think it would cover any costs. More likely end up being a rock on a shelf in your home that eventually gets lost."

"You're such a party pooper. Why not dream big?"

"Because I'm a realist?" He kept his eyes glued to the signs ahead, informing him where to park. Life might be more fun if he were an idealist like Bree.

"Well, I'm going in with the intention of finding something amazing just to prove you wrong." Bree had her door open almost before he had the car in park.

"Right." He started to get out and then hesitated.

She wanted a diamond.

He had a diamond ... in his pocket ... this very minute.

Was this God giving him an opportunity, or was he reading too much into the situation?

"You coming?" Bree stood on the sidewalk and tapped her foot.

"Yep. One more minute. I thought I had a hat in here."

Making sure he kept his hands low, he dug the box out of his pocket and wiggled the ring free, slipping it back into the shelter of his shorts. His mama would at least be proud that he was going in prepared, as she'd told him to do.

Inside the welcome center, they stepped up to the counter to pay their entrance fees and rent a few tools to use out in the crater. This would be their last few minutes in air conditioning, and the line moved much too quickly. Bree's smile stretched wide as she accepted a few little shovels and a sifter from the ranger behind the desk.

If nothing else, he made her happy today. After all the tears yesterday, he hadn't been sure he could do that anymore. She led the way out into the sunshine again, and he pulled his cap low over his eyes and followed.

"What about over there?" Bree pointed past a few families, some of whom had pop-up tents blocking a few of the bright rays, and aimed herself toward the middle of the thirty-seven-and-a-half-acre plowed field.

Because why stay close to the edge where he wouldn't have to walk as far? He followed, his fingers fiddling with the jewelry beneath the khaki fabric on his legs. Would he be able to do this? She still hadn't said a word about last night. Where exactly did he stand in her life?

Only a few feet into the field, he realized one oversight. The rains from the night before had turned the normally dry area into a big muddy mess. A layer of muck covered the bottoms of both shoes, and each step was harder to take. Lovely. An already awful idea just got worse.

"Ready to dig?" She held out the bigger shovel to him. "I figured if we go deeper than others before us, we're more likely to come across something."

"I didn't bring an excavator, Bree. Just how deep are you

wanting me to go?" The wood of the shovel was rough on his hands.

"I just need you to get it started for me. As wet as things are, it shouldn't be hard." With her head tilted that way, her ponytail swinging jauntily, she looked more like a teenager than a twenty-one-year-old woman. "Please?"

"Let's do this." He jabbed the spade into the dark ground and scooped out as big a pile as he could. Might not be impressive by others' standards, but it made Bree happy.

After he'd dug out several more heaps, she knelt on the earth, not giving a care to what it would do to her bright pink capris. "Here goes nothing."

Fifteen minutes later, he sank down on his haunches beside her. As meticulous as she was in searching through each grain of dirt, this could take a while. She moved her finger through the muck as if each glob were precious, and it mesmerized him.

"Do you remember what the various colors were they showed us? I know they said most diamonds out here wouldn't be clear." She glanced over her shoulder. "I'm basically looking for anything the slightest bit shiny, right?"

"I guess. You could go use the water to sift it even more. That's what a lot of people do."

She sighed. "I guess I figured maybe they'd be just as easy to find without water."

"Up to you. This was your idea, after all." He pointed to some people simply walking around, their gaze on the ground. "The ranger said something about the possibility of some having washed up close to the surface last night due to the hard rains. We could try that if you're tired of this."

"You're just hoping I'll give up."

"Nope." He rose and offered her a hand. "Simply trying to help."

Bree hesitated a moment before accepting his assistance. He pulled a bit harder than she expected, and she planted her hand on his chest to keep from a total collision. Their eyes met and held for a short eternity before he cleared his throat and stepped back. Muddy fingerprints remained over his heart, an outward sign of the war inside her own chest. He cleared his throat.

Right.

What were they doing again? Diamonds. Looking for shiny rocks.

"Which way should we walk?"

He pointed toward a corner behind her. "Maybe that way? Doesn't seem to be as many people over there."

"All right." She brushed off her pants, though the knees remained stained, and started moving, one slow step at a time, as her eyes studied the ground around them for anything that might remotely resemble a rock worth something.

"Oops!" One of her flip-flops remained behind when she stepped forward. This mud was thick.

"You trying to play Cinderella?" Nathan retrieved the flip-flop from the muck and held it out.

"Why? You know where I can find a Prince Charming?" The remark slipped out before she thought better of it.

But he just shrugged, a little lift of a brow, not saying a word.

"Okay, then." She slid her shoe back on. "Back to it, I guess."

Nathan lugged their tools as he walked beside her, quiet and strong. It was obvious he hadn't wanted to come, but here he was, not one word of complaint. Well, she could offer up a few, but they wouldn't be about the heat or what a ridiculous idea this had been.

No, she was going crazy wondering about everything that had happened the night before. And every time she drew close to forgiveness, she pulled back again. Because even though the words he'd whispered in the middle of the night had been perfect, they'd also been missing one thing.

Another proposal.

A girl couldn't just offer to move on and forget she should've been married a week before. Hoops needed to be jumped through. Or, in this case, fields sifted and dug up.

"Anything?" He nudged a particularly large lump of earth out of the way with his toe.

"Not yet."

His mama's words about not giving up on him—and eloping—were sweet enough. But she wasn't about to run off and elope with someone who hadn't actually said he wanted to marry her. Saying she was the best choice for him was all well and good, but the best choice for what?

Suggesting they come search for diamonds had been more about buying time with him than actually wanting to prove him wrong. Although she wouldn't complain about finding an actual diamond either. No. She just couldn't wrap her head around what might happen when he dropped her off in Memphis in a few hours. Wasn't ready to face it yet.

So, here they were. Traipsing through a hot, muddy field, still not talking. Walking in circles, figuratively and physically.

"Look here." Nathan knelt a few feet away. When had he gotten so far ahead of her?

She crouched down and followed the direction of his finger. A tiny stone glimmered in the sunlight. Really?

It was no bigger than a match head, slightly shiny, though nothing like the diamond that had sparkled on her engagement ring … before … Instead, this rock looked more like a small bit of lead, round on the edges, and faintly translucent.

Bree pinched it between her fingers. "Do you think it is? How did you even spot such a small thing?"

"I happened to look down at the right time, I guess." He leaned close as he studied it too. So close she could see the beginnings of whiskers growing on his cheeks.

"I guess we can ask them about it in the office on our way out, huh?" She let her eyes wander over to his.

"Guess so." He didn't blink for several seconds. "Did you want to keep looking for more?"

She ducked her head, frustrated with the tension sizzling between them. "Sure."

Was that disappointment that crossed his face? Frustration? She couldn't even read him anymore.

Farther across the field they trod. The sun was merciless in its beating. But if she complained about being hot, he'd be able to remind her of his warning earlier.

She kicked at a clod in front of her, splattering her pants and scattering larger rocks. Might as well be her dreams, the way this was going. Was she only prolonging the inevitable?

"Bree, look." Nathan once again knelt a few feet away.

Another tiny rock that might or might not be a diamond? If it was, why wasn't she excited? This had been her idea, after all. But the longer it went on, the harder she found it to pretend things were normal.

She lowered herself beside the man who was a bigger treasure than anything in this field and offered a small smile—all she had. "Find something else?"

"How about this?"

The sunlight shot into several rays and colors as it shone through the stone in his hand. The stone attached to a gold ring. A ring that looked very familiar.

Was the sun brighter? The heat less oppressive? But if everything was better, why was it harder to draw a full breath?

"Bree, I messed up. Canceling our wedding was the worst mistake I ever made." He didn't meet her eyes but studied the ground as if another diamond would pop up simply from the intensity of his stare. "I'm not going to be perfect. I know that. I've proved it a million times over. But I'd love another chance if you're willing to give me one."

She grabbed both of his hands in her own, not saying anything until his silvery blue gaze met hers. "I'd love another chance."

A breath whooshed out of him so big she wondered there was any air left. "Really?"

"Really." With a squeeze of his fingers, she winked. "Now, can I have my real diamond back?"

That one corner of his lips tilted up, and he slid the ring back on her finger. Her nails were dirty, and her polish had come off days before, but she didn't care. With the sparkle back where it belonged, her hands looked better than ever.

"You're not just saying that for the ring, are you?" He poked her shoulder as she admired her hand.

"What? No!" And she pushed up on her heels enough to press a kiss to his lips. "I'm saying it because what you said last night is exactly how I feel about you too."

He stood and pulled her to her feet. As he looked around, a chuckle emerged from his chest. "This may officially be my favorite state park now."

"Let's turn in our digging equipment and get out of here. We've got some phone calls to make."

"I like the sound of that plan."

As he returned the shovels, she showed their shiny find to a ranger and confirmed it was a tiny diamond. Could this day get any better? Best end to a road trip ever. They scrubbed their hands and headed out.

"Want to call people from here or wait until we're in an air-conditioned restaurant for lunch?"

"Ooh. The second one. That way, I can just savor the knowledge all to myself for a little longer."

"Whatever you say." He opened her car door and helped her in.

"They're going to be excited, right? I mean, your mom did say she wouldn't mind us eloping."

He laughed. "She said that, but I don't know how much she actually meant it. Something tells me she'd love to be able to go to a real wedding. With two boys, she'll never get to actually be in on the planning more than she was when you let her in last year."

"And now we can't even have that wedding. Everything was canceled and returned. Except the dresses. Not to mention the date is already past." Worry stained the edges of her happiness.

"Hey." He wove his fingers through hers. "We've made it this far. We'll work it out."

But what would they have to do to work it out? How much longer would she have to wait to become Mrs. Nathan Hart?

23

"There's no waiting in Tennessee after you get your marriage license. We could actually stop by the county clerk on the way through Memphis and pick one up. Maybe even find a justice of the peace or a preacher who's available." Bree scrolled through the other requirements listed on the website, excitement replacing the earlier hunger in her belly. She could be married as early as tonight!

"And you'd be okay with that?" Nathan finished off his fourth taco. "I mean, you wouldn't have a nice dress or flowers or anything."

"But I'd have you."

That raised the corner of his lips. "Yes. But none of our parents. And you wouldn't get to have Skye and Katie as bridesmaids."

Bree slumped, her elbows on the table, fists holding up her cheeks. How badly did she want her best girls there? The idea of making sure Katie caught the bouquet still made her grin. But something told her Katie and Camden wouldn't need that bit of superstition to find their way to the altar in the near future.

"You want all those people there, don't you?" Nathan pointed at her with a chip he'd snitched from her hardly-touched plate.

"I mean, of course I do. But I want you more." A bit of whine crept into her words, but she couldn't help it. It'd been forever since he proposed the first time. Well over a year.

"How about let's talk to our parents and see what they think?" He raised a brow. "If they give their blessing, we'll figure it out on the way to Memphis."

"I bet they will. They've all expected us to be married almost as long as we have." She set her purse on the table and pulled out her phone.

"But we're going to listen if they don't, right?" He had her pausing in scrolling through her contacts.

A big part of her wanted to argue. They were both old enough to get married without permission. But she also knew he was right. She gave a brisk nod and then pressed the button to call her mom.

"Mom, how long would it take for you to get to Tennessee?" Bree pressed her phone to her ear, nachos only half eaten in front of her. She hadn't been able to wait any longer.

"Well, that depends. It only takes about half an hour to get to the Kentucky state line, but I assume you want me to come farther than that." Her mom's voice held touches of laughter. "What's going on?"

"Remember how I told you about the trip being ... changed? And how Nathan ended up staying in Dallas too?"

"Ye-es." The humor was gone.

"Well, we've sort of worked things out again, and we're hoping we can get married as soon as possible."

"Breanna Grace Henley, you can't be serious."

Bree blinked. That hadn't been what she expected. No sounds of rejoicing or promises of coming down later that day.

"Of course I'm serious. Why would I make something like that up?"

"Is he with you right now?"

Bree held the phone out to make sure she really was talking to the woman she'd called. "Yes. He's right here beside me. We're stopped for lunch in Little Rock."

Mumbles sounded on her mom's end, probably explaining to Dad what was going on. Which meant he'd be one up on Bree. A deeper voice sounded in the background, as well as some static, like the phone was being shuffled.

"Bree, honey. Can you put us on speaker phone?" Dad's voice was much calmer though there was still a note of caution.

She motioned Nathan closer to her and pressed the little icon where they could both hear. "We're here, Dad."

"I hear you guys have come to an understanding."

"We're engaged again, Daddy." Bree glanced down at the ring once more to make sure she wasn't dreaming.

"Bree, it's too fast." Mom's voice interrupted before her dad could reply.

"Too fast? Mom, we were supposed to be married a week ago. How can this be too fast?"

"Because neither one of you have proven yourselves adult enough to handle marriage." Mom was in her take-no-nonsense mood. But Bree could play that game just as well.

"How do you figure?"

"He called things off out of nowhere, never explained why, and then, suddenly, after only a few days of playing tourist together, you're both okay with moving forward again? That doesn't sound like good decision-making skills."

"What your mother means—"

Nathan cut in. "We understand. May I speak for a moment?"

A pause, and then her dad affirmed they'd listen.

"I was stupid, sir." Nathan ran a hand over the back of his neck. "I was trying to protect Bree from something I thought might happen down the road. You see, my father left my mother when I was seven, and I was afraid ... well, that it might be hereditary. But several people have pointed out that I am not my father, and that I have a great support system, and I don't plan to turn into him.

"I've asked your daughter's forgiveness. And now, I'm asking yours too. I know I left you all with a huge mess. And for that, I'm terribly sorry. I had no idea."

"I appreciate your apology." Dad cleared his throat. "That does make me feel better. But I'm also going to offer some advice."

"We're listening, sir." Nathan covered Bree's hand as her mouth opened to protest. "We need advice from couples like you so we can do just as well in our marriage."

Bree squeezed her lips together. If she was going to trust this man enough to marry him and promise to live up to those verses in the Bible, she needed to start allowing him to lead now. She gave a little nod and rested her head on his shoulder.

"It sounds like you've discovered some deep-rooted issues from your past. I'm not saying Bree won't have her own. Every person comes to a relationship with his or her own history. But that being said, it might do you both some good to have some more counseling before moving forward. This time, bring up those worries and concerns you've unearthed and get some advice and ways to prevent such problems from arising in your marriage."

Her dad's advice was sound, of course. Though Bree hated

to admit it, because it meant even longer before she could be Nathan's wife. As if he could hear her thoughts, he squeezed her hand.

"Thank you for trusting us enough and loving us enough to want the best for us," Nathan spoke for both of them. Just as well. Bree wasn't sure she could get any sound out yet.

"Thank you for being willing to listen. We love you both, and we want to see you start out with the best chances at success that you possibly can." Bree could picture her dad with a bit of a twinkle in his eyes as he said it. And Mom would be agreeing with him, even if it was grudgingly.

"We'll talk soon." Nathan ended the call and wrapped Bree up in his arms.

"So much for not having to say goodbye again." The words were just over a whisper as Bree buried her face in Nathan's neck.

"Hey." He nudged her with a knuckle. "Just a few more times. Then we can stay together for always. I promise. And we both know your dad's right."

"I know." She groaned. "But that doesn't mean I'm happy about it."

"Want to call my mom now? She's going to be ecstatic."

"Let's send her a picture." The thought of surprising the woman who would be her mother-in-law perked her back up a little. She held out her hand, and he obligingly snapped the pic and texted it to Mama Hart.

Not thirty seconds later, Nathan's phone rang. He winked at her and switched it to speaker just as his mama's voice came through in a squeal.

"Please tell me that's what I think it is."

"Well, it's not the diamond we found at Crater of Diamonds State Park this morning." Bree laughed.

"I'm so excited I could spit!" Mama's voice was so loud several of the other customers looked over with curious glances. "When? How long do I have to wait to finally have my daughter?"

"We're not sure yet." Nathan gathered their things, and they walked out as they continued the call. "Bree's parents recommended we get some more counseling after everything we've gone through. Not to mention the revelations I've had concerning Dad and wanting to make sure I don't turn out like him."

"I know you won't, honey." Mama's affirmations warmed his heart almost as much as having Bree's hand in his once more. "But I guess I agree. Just don't wait too long, huh?"

"We won't wait any longer than we have to. Both of us are ready after all this time." He helped Bree into the car and then went around to his side. "Hey. We're about to start driving again, but I wanted to let you know because you were hoping this would happen."

"Never gave up hope of it, hon. And I'm so pleased. Y'all drive safe."

"Yes, ma'am." He started the car. "I'll let you know when I get home."

"Please do."

He ended the call and then leaned over and kissed his fiancée. Things might not have ended exactly the way Josh hoped, but they were ending pretty sweet. Time to get this show on the road. The sooner they got back to reality, the sooner they could work out all the details and make them happen.

"Should we apologize to Josh and Katie and Skye for being

mad about them setting us up this week?" Bree wove her fingers through his as he merged onto the interstate toward Memphis.

"Nope. They don't need any more reason to gloat than they already have."

Bree giggled and his heart danced along. Considering how things had been between them last Saturday, he'd never expected to hear such a sweet sound again. Yes. Things were looking up despite facing several months of a long-distance relationship.

She picked up her phone and tapped away at something. He didn't mind. Contentment was a cloak around him, and he found he couldn't be annoyed at much—not even the crazy afternoon traffic.

A few minutes later, his phone notified him of something to do with social media. A glance Bree's direction showed her covering laughter with her hands. Hm.

"Why do you look so suspicious right after my phone *dings*?"

"I was updating social media with some pictures from our week." Bree kept her eyes glued to her screen.

"Did I get a say in what was posted?"

"Nope."

"Bree!"

"If you don't like the way they look, maybe you should smile more." She pressed a quick kiss to his cheek and then started catching up on her friends' posts.

"Seriously?" Nathan muttered, but he didn't protest anymore.

"That ornament I bought is going to be extra special now."

"Well, that was a sudden change in subject." He shook his head. "What made you think of that?"

"I saw a Christmas in July post despite the fact that it's still June for a couple more days." She shrugged. "But now we'll be able to hang it on our first Christmas tree together. Assuming we're married by then."

"We will be if I get any say in the matter." He waggled his eyebrows. "Who knew you were so sentimental about souvenirs?"

"Well, at least I didn't bring back a souvenir like Katie got on our last trip." Bree smirked.

"You better not have." Nathan shot her a glare, although it wasn't a serious one. "I don't think it would be appropriate, among other things, for you to bring a new boyfriend back from the trip where you got engaged to your ex-fiancé."

"Okay, fine. I'll keep my old boyfriend." She gave him a playful pinch.

Nathan scowled and rubbed the spot. "If you're not careful, he'll be damaged goods."

"Nah. Just broken in good."

She returned to her scrolling but not for long. "Aw. Speaking of Katie, look at this."

Holding her screen so he could see, too, she pointed to a photo of Katie and Camden.

Nathan huffed. "I still can't believe you and Skye basically forced them together on that trip."

"They're so perfect together." Bree let out a happy sigh. "I mean, look at them. He looks at her the way you look at me. I bet there will be wedding bells for them soon. I can't wait."

"Think she'll let you wear a maroon dress with a lace top?" Nathan couldn't help but think back to a few nights before and their date at the tower. Her dress had been amazing, and he wouldn't complain about seeing her in it again.

"I don't care. I'll wear whatever she wants because it'll be her day." Bree leaned her head on Nathan's shoulder. "I love weddings."

"How about you let Camden propose before you start planning their wedding, huh?" Nathan risked giving her a quick kiss on her temple.

"Yeah, I know. But a girl can be happy for her friends, right?"

"Right." He nudged her. "What about Skye? She didn't find her happily ever after on your trip."

"No. I thought for a few days that maybe she and Camden's cousin would couple off too, but she has this thing where she never lets herself get too serious with a guy. Something to do with not being ready to settle down and fear of getting bored." Bree shrugged. "But I'm still holding out hope for her."

"Maybe she'll meet someone back home."

"Oh, she's not at home." Bree pulled up Skye's profile on her phone and flashed him her latest post. "She's in Colorado."

"Colorado? What's she doing there?"

"From what I can tell, helping her sister with her wedding planning business. Before she went home, she said something about her dad giving her an ultimatum—either she found a job or he took away her convertible. And you know how she loves that car."

Nathan rolled his eyes. "So, I guess her dad is counting her helping her sister as a job?"

"For now. We'll see what happens."

"Even if she does find someone in Colorado, I doubt they could be as happy together as we are."

"You think? I don't know." Bree closed her eyes. "I like to think there's enough happiness to go around for everyone."

"There's the optimist I know and love." He pressed another kiss to her head.

"Hard not to be an optimist when God keeps blessing me

so richly." She held her hand up, moving the ring back and forth to glimmer in the sunshine.

"Not as richly as He blessed me when you allowed your honeymoon for one to turn into a road trip for two."

"And a road trip for two is the only kind I ever want to take again."

AUTHOR'S NOTE

Dear Reader,

This is not the story I wrote originally.

My first plan was to have Bree and Nathan married at the end of Book One, and this be their honeymoon trip. But my (very wise) editor reminded me no one wants to read a story about two newlyweds who fight the whole week. So, back to the drawing board I went. And this is what happened. While I was able to keep a few scenes here and there, most of this is new. You can't write about newlyweds the same way you write about an estranged couple, for more than one reason.

Despite the rough start, I love how this book turned out. Having to make Nathan the bad guy at the end of Book One just about killed me, but I like to think he was fully redeemed in Dallas—or maybe a few chapters later in Arkansas.

For the record, I have explored a few of those places in Dallas myself, including the Sixth Floor Museum. And we've been stuck at the DFW airport waiting for tornadoes to ease up so flights could take off again, too. That was a long day! I've also enjoyed the scorching sun beating down on me while searching for the ever-elusive diamond at the Crater of Diamonds State Park in Arkansas. Unlike Bree, I didn't come away with a diamond of any kind.

I hope you've enjoyed this second roadtrip romance in my series. Next up is Skye's story, and I can't wait for you to get to know her even better. In that one, you head to Boulder, Colorado, so get ready! Until then, if you enjoyed this story, it would be a huge blessing to me if you could leave a review for it and share it with friends. I appreciate each and every one of my readers.

Love, Amy

DISCUSSION QUESTIONS

1. What would your dream vacation look like? Would you prefer a cruise like Nathan was planning, a trip to the city with all the sights like Bree wanted, or something else?

2. Trips don't always go as planned, much like life in general, not to mention marriage. Have you ever had life throw you a curveball like Bree and Nathan did with the hurricane? Do you think it was good practice for their future marriage?

3. Bree and Nathan are both hurting from their breakup, but won't admit it to each other. Do you think they could have had a better week if they had simply talked it out at the beginning?

4. Bree and Nathan's friends had good intentions when they set the couple up on the trip, but they didn't think everything through. As the week goes on, several repercussions come to mind as they talk to the couple on the phone. Do you think it was

worth the risk? Would you try something like this with your friends?

5. Bree admitted she had thought about deleting the pictures of Nathan from her phone, but hadn't been able to do that yet. Do you have mementos from past romantic relationships or friendships that didn't work out? What is the advantage or disadvantage of keeping physical reminders?

6. At the Sixth Floor Museum, Bree is touched by the story of JFK's assassination, but Nathan is thinking with his more analytical mind. Have you ever put yourself in someone else's shoes like Bree did? Or are you more like Nathan? Do you think one is better than the other?

7. Nathan gets outside his comfort zone when he takes an Uber to find Bree. And then he puts his fear of heights aside to ride to the top of Reunion Tower. Have you ever loved someone so much that you'd be willing to take a risk you never thought you'd take?

8. Bree doesn't worry about how she'll pay off the debt she's accruing on this unplanned trip, and Nathan considers that rather stupid. Even though she has a plan to be able to earn the money, it's not foolproof. Is her view of money better or Nathan's? Or do you think they'll be able to find a middle ground?

9. Nathan is worried about turning out like his dad did, leaving a wife behind to raise their children by herself? Was that truly a legitimate concern, or should he have seen sooner what his mom reminds him? Have you ever let someone from your past

influence a decision about your future in a way you shouldn't have?

10. When Nathan and Bree announce they're back together, her parents caution them to wait a bit longer before proceeding with the marriage. Have you ever had to wait for something you wanted to happen? Did it make it better?

ABOUT THE AUTHOR

Amy R Anguish grew up a preacher's kid, and in spite of having lived in seven different states that are all south of the Mason Dixon line, she is not a football fan. Currently, she resides in Tennessee with her husband, daughter, and son, and usually a bossy cat or two. Amy has an English degree from Freed-Hardeman University that she intends to use to glorify God, and she wants her stories to show that while Christians face real struggles, it can still work out for good.

Follow her at http://abitofanguish.weebly.com or http://www.facebook.com/amyanguishauthor

Or https://twitter.com/amy_r_anguish

Learn more about her books at https://www.pinterest.com/msguish/my-books/

And check out the YouTube channel she does with two other authors, Once Upon a Page (https://www.youtube.com/channel/UCEiu-jq-KE-VMIjbtmGLbJA)

ALSO BY AMY R. ANGUISH

Love in Any Season

A novella collection that includes

The Missing Piece – by Amy R. Anguish

Beth Norton and Tommy England grew up together with best-friend moms who had a love of quilting and a business celebrating the craft. When high school ended, though, so did Beth and Tommy's friendship.

When Tommy moves back after seven years and his mother's death, he can't understand why Beth is so angry with him. Helping Beth and her mother stabilize the finances of the business, they're forced to work together. As Tommy sorts through his mother's things, he finds an unfinished quilt, and it turns into a joint project.

With each stitch taken, they work toward more than just a completed blanket.

Get your copy here:

https://scrivenings.link/loveinanyseason

Destination: ~~Fun~~ Romance

It's not every day you bring a boyfriend back as a souvenir.

Katie Wilhite is ready to settle into her new job as a librarian now that college is through, but friends Bree and Skye want one more girls' trip, and when Bree insists this is her bachelorette fling, Katie agrees. What she didn't agree to was allowing fun and flighty Skye to dictate the itinerary or for her anxiety to kick in harder than ever … right in front of a cute guy.

Camden Malone had no idea when he agreed to be the voice of reason on his cousin Ryan's vacation that the trip wouldn't stay in New Orleans as planned. But when Ryan plots with Skye so that the guys can tag along with the girls all week, he isn't nearly as upset as he should be. Not with Katie's fiery temper and flashing eyes intriguing him more by the minute.

Can Katie relax enough to trust Camden and a possible future, or will she continue to push him away as only a vacation fling? And can Camden move past a rocky history of his own to be able to jump into a better future? For a trip that was supposed to be all about fun, there's a lot of romance going around.

Get your copy here:

https://scrivenings.link/destinationromance

No Place Like Home

Can love secure Adrian's wandering heart?

Roots are overrated, at least to someone like Adrian Stewart, preacher's kid, who has never lived anywhere longer than six years. That's why her job with MidUSLogIn Inc., is so perfect for her—lots of travel, and staying nowhere long enough to have it feel like home. But when work takes her to Memphis, closer to her family for the first time in years and in the same small office as Grayson Roberts, she starts to question her job, her lack of home, and even her memories of her rocky past with the church.

Gray is intrigued by Adrian from the moment he sees her, and he's determined to get to the bottom of why this girl, who loves old movies and hums when she works, won't go to church with him. As they grow closer, he wants more too, but how can he convince her to stay in Memphis when she doesn't believe in home—or God? Can he use his own broken past to break through hers?

Get your copy here:

https://scrivenings.link/noplacelikehome

Candy Cane Wishes and Saltwater Dreams

A novella collection that includes

Mistletoe Make-believe by Amy R. Anguish

Charlie Hill's family thinks his daughter Hailey needs a mom–to the point they won't get off his back until he finds her one. Desperate to be free from their nagging, he asks a stranger to pretend she's his girlfriend during the holidays.

When romance author Samantha Arwine takes a working vacation to

St. Simon's Island over Christmas, she never dreamed she'd be involved in a real-life romance. Are the sparks between her and Charlie real?

Or is her imagination over-acting … again?

Get your copy here:

https://scrivenings.link/candycanewishes

Saving Grace

Michelle Wilson's one goal in life was to become a top journalist at the local paper back in her hometown of Cedar Springs, AR. But on the way to bringing that dream to reality, a life-changing wreck interrupts Michelle's plans and adds an orphaned baby into the mix. Now, she has tough decisions ahead—did God put her in that accident to save baby Grace? And if so, why is it so hard to convince everyone else she should be the baby's new mommy?

Greg Marshall has been Michelle's best friend his whole life. He's thrilled she's moving back home, but not so sure about her sudden desire to be a single mom. His feelings for her have grown through the years, but she's never seemed to notice. Can he help Michelle with the adoption and grow their relationship at the same time?

Get your copy here:

https://scrivenings.link/savinggrace

Faith and Hope

Hope needs more hope. Faith needs more faith. They both need a whole lot of love.

Two sisters. One summer. Multiple problems.

Younger sister Hope has lost her job, her car, and her boyfriend all in one day. Her well-laid plans for life have gone sideways, as has her hope in God.

Older sister Faith is finally getting her dream-come-true after years of struggles and prayers. But when her mom talks her into letting

Hope move in for the summer, will the stress turn her dream into a nightmare? Is her faith in God strong enough to handle everything?

For two sisters who haven't gotten along in years, this summer together could be a disaster, or it could lead them to a closer relationship with each other and God. Can they overcome all life is throwing at them? Or is this going to destroy their relationship for good?

Get your copy here:

https://scrivenings.link/faithandhope

An Unexpected Legacy

When Chad Manning introduces himself to Jessica Garcia at her favorite smoothie shop, it's like he stepped out of one of her romance novels. But as she tentatively walks into a relationship with this man of her dreams, secrets from their past threaten to shatter their already fragile bond. Chad and Jessica must struggle to figure out if their relationship has a chance or if there is nothing between them but a love of smoothies.

Get your copy here:

https://scrivenings.link/anunexpectedlegacy

Bentonsport: A Christmas Story

by Lisa Schnedler

What if you found the love of your life right in your hometown—in another century?

For Bentonsport Academy Headmaster Thomas Barton, Christmas emphasizes his loneliness. He has given up hope of discovering a woman to share his heart and life and plans to return to his hometown for the holidays. But when his friend's preposterous prophecy comes true, he finds himself having traveled not by train, but through time, from 1869, to Bentonsport today! Now he must navigate a modern world for the two weeks before Christmas and discover what he was sent to find.

Baker Sarah Peterson has everything she wants in the small historic town of modern-day Bentonsport—everything but a man with whom to share her dreams and future. And, in a town of under fifty residents, where's she going to encounter a soulmate? But when Thomas walks into her bakery, seemingly odd and out of place, but handsome and charming, she finds herself hoping something special might happen this Christmas.

Bentonsport—two different eras in one special town, two lonely persons, and one miraculous Christmas ...

Get your copy here:

https://scrivenings.link/bentonsport

Forever Home

by Hope Toler Dougherty

With a fulfilling job and a home of her own, former foster child, Merritt Hastings, relishes her stable, respectable life. Dreaming for more is a sure way for heartache. When a contested will turns her world upside down, she must revaluate what's important to her, what's worth fighting for, and what's worth sacrificing.

Patience has never been Sam Daniels' strong suit with his history of acting quickly and asking questions later, and he's ready for changes in his life...now. Too bad the plans for acquiring a radio station didn't include a contract. Now he's out of a job, out of a radio station, and out of prospects.

While his life is in flux, at least he can help Merritt steady hers, or will he rush in and overstep ...again?

Will the sparks flying between these two opposites lead to a happily-ever-after or heartbreak for both?

Get your copy here:

https://scrivenings.link/foreverhome

Stay up-to-date on your favorite books and authors with our free e-newsletters.

ScriveningsPress.com